Praise for

the oracle of dating

"*The Oracle of Dating* is, without a doubt, the cutest book
I've read so far this year, and a fantastic start to a new series!"
—*Lauren's Crammed Bookshelf*

"I absolutely ate up this light, amusing tale of romance and friendship.…
Read it for a positive spin on girl friendship, for the spunky narrator,
for some smoking sexual tension (hey, this is Harlequin, after all!) that
doesn't cross the line, and, of course, for a tale of first love."
—Kinnelon Library Teen Blog

"*The Oracle of Dating* is a quick, fun read with a witty lead character."
—*The Lip Gloss Chronicles*

"It's fun, wonderfully lighthearted, and the whole Oracle element
puts an entirely new twist on the typical young adult romance…
it even gives some pretty insightful and useful dating advice."
—*Obsessed!*

"An adorable read. It took me back to the best moments of high school,
made me feel the romance and just took me out of life for a while."
—*My Reading Room*

D1517904

Also by Allison van Diepen
from Harlequin Teen

THE ORACLE OF DATING

the oracle rebounds

Allison van Diepen

HARLEQUIN®
TEEN

HARLEQUIN®
TEEN

ISBN-13: 978-0-373-21021-3

THE ORACLE REBOUNDS

Recycling programs
for this product may
not exist in your area.

www.HarlequinTEEN.com

Printed in U.S.A.

For two special guys in my life, Jeremy and Nate.

And for cheering the Oracle on, a big thank-you
to Mary-Theresa Hussey, Natashya Wilson and Elizabeth Mazer
at Harlequin Teen, and my agent, Ashley Grayson.

What are the warning signs that your boyfriend is about to break up with you?

a) He's avoiding your calls.

b) He keeps canceling on you.

c) You catch him getting cozy with another girl.

d) He spends more time with his friends than with you.

Correct answer? Any of the above. Warning signs vary. And if you're really unlucky, there aren't any.

one

Happily ever after is meant to last forever, right? Well, my happily ever after lasts five months, three weeks and two days. Then Jared drops a bomb.

"I need to take a step back, Kayla. I have to figure some things out right now."

I stop listening after the "step back" part. I feel like I'm sinking through the floor. Jared is *the one,* isn't he? This can't be happening.

He's watching me. "You're not saying anything."

"I'm chewing my pizza so I don't choke."

"Oh."

I swallow my food. *Keep it together,* I tell myself. Having a public meltdown will only make this worse. "What do you want me to say?"

"I don't know. Just that you understand."

"I don't."

I don't and I don't want to. Why can't this be any other Saturday night at Colonnade Pizza? I must've misheard him. He can't be breaking up with me.... God, he's so beautiful, with his curly dark hair falling over his forehead, and his blue eyes so tortured. He's talking again. "Ever since I didn't get that scholarship to art school, I've had to think about what I'm going to do with my life."

"I get that, but how does that lead to you dumping me?" And then it hits me. He must've met another girl. The familiarity between us, the ease of us knowing each other so well, no longer excites him. Before he can answer my question, I throw it out there. "Is there someone else?"

His eyes widen. "Didn't you hear anything I said?"

"Of course I did. I'm just asking."

"You're the only girl and that's the truth." He sighs. "I've been too into you these past few months. I haven't been focusing enough on my art. If I'd put more effort into my portfolio, I might've gotten that scholarship. I was counting on it, and now I'm not sure what I'll do. This is an important time in my life and I've been spending more time thinking about you than my own future."

He's talking, talking, blah, blah, blah…

And all I'm hearing is that I'm being dumped.

"Kayla, are you okay?"

My eyes fill up. My throat is closing. I'm either discovering a new food allergy or having my heart broken. "I'm… surprised, that's all."

"I'm not saying this is permanent. I don't know."

I'll wait for you, Jared. I'll give you time. Whatever you need. But I can't say it. Pride doesn't let me. "You're making a big mistake, don't you see that? I'm not just going to wait around for you. It's…insulting!"

He shrugs helplessly. That look in his eyes—it's killing me. He looks sad, and I have a sneaking suspicion it's for *me*.

Dumping me is one thing. Pitying me is another. He's so crossed the line.

"Maybe it's better if it *is* permanent," I say, unable to keep the edge out of my voice. "Teen relationships only have a thirteen percent chance of being long-term anyway."

"That's the Oracle talking, not you."

"Yeah, well, we're one and the same. I'm going to move on, Jared. I'm not going to sit around waiting for you."

He nods gravely. "I understand."

I blink. Can he let me go just like that? After spending half a year with him, after telling him I love him, this is humiliating. Didn't he promise to love me forever? What about that?

"I'm going." I slide out of the booth.

He grabs my arm. "Kayla…"

"What? Do you have anything more to say?"

"I guess…not." He lets go of my arm. He can't even look at me anymore.

"Bye." And I'm gone.

In the blink of an eye, everything is different. I ride the subway in a daze, torn between tears and hysterical laughter. It's over. OVER.

As the Oracle of Dating, I should have seen this coming. Sure, Jared has been acting a little weird recently, but I thought that was because he didn't get the scholarship to art school. I'd hated to see him so disappointed, and I'd done everything I could to cheer him up. He seemed to be feeling better the past few days, like he'd finally accepted it and turned a corner. Maybe the real reason his mood had improved was because he'd made the decision to send me to Dumpsville.

I remember reading in one of Mom's relationship books that sometimes when people feel powerless in their lives, they dump their significant other because that's one part of their lives they do have control over. Worse, sometimes they blame their partner for their problems. Maybe that's what Jared is doing. *"I've been too into you these past few months."* Aren't you supposed to be into the person you're dating?

Well, Jared, if I'd known it was a problem for you, I wouldn't have been so damned fantastic!

Whatever, he made his decision. I have to move on. There are lots of cute guys around. It's not like I haven't noticed them. I have!

Half an hour later, I get home. I live on a quiet street in Midwood, Brooklyn, with big old trees that shed branches whenever there's heavy rain or wind. I've lived in this old brownstone ever since I can remember. Dad left us the house when he and Mom divorced, though apparently he made Mom buy him out. Since my sister, Tracey, is ten years older than me and lives in Manhattan, it's just me, Mom and my stepdad, a Swedish theologian named Erland.

Mom's car is gone, which is good because I don't feel like talking right now. I just want to go to my room and bawl. First I have to get past Erland, who's in the living room watching PBS. I close the door quietly and creep toward the stairs.

"What are you doing home so early?"

Great. I go back into the living room. "Jared..." My chin quivers. "H-he b-broke up w-with me."

"I'm sorry to hear this," he says with his thick Swedish-chef accent. "Can I offer you a hug?"

I almost laugh at the formal offer, but I go to receive his hug. "Thanks." I sit beside him on the couch. "I don't know why I'm crying. It's his loss!"

He chuckles. "That's true. And you are both very young, too young to get serious."

"I know." The Oracle is always advising teen girls not to get too serious about their relationships. I've seen so many of them devastated when their boyfriends break up with them. The truth is, many guys just aren't ready for anything serious at our age. Knowing that, I'd shied away from relationships myself, since the odds of them working are extremely low. And then I met Jared, and my good sense went out the window. I thought we had a once-in-a-lifetime connection, a connection worth taking a risk for. And now...Dumpsville.

"What I'm saying is," Erland continues in his slow, professorly way, "as we get older, we learn more about what qualities are important to us in a partner."

"I know you're right. It just hurts." I've read that heartbreak is an accepted cause of death in some South American countries. I don't want to die. What a waste to die over a guy!

Erland hands me some tissue. "I had my heart broken when I was young. The girl was named Hannah...or maybe it was Krista."

"She broke your heart and you can't even remember her name?"

"It appears that way." He laughs. "She was such a beautiful girl, and she promised me she'd always be mine. I thought we might marry one day. And then one week before our prom, she broke up with me. I later heard she attended with another boy, one of the school's best hockey players."

"That's harsh. I bet she'd regret it if she knew you were one of the world's top Martin Luther scholars."

Erland blushes. "I doubt she would have appreciated my career in theology. We were not well matched, she and I, and in time I realized that. If I had stayed with her I would've had a very different life. I will always be glad that she broke up with me because otherwise I never would have met your mother, who is truly my soul mate."

Erland believes in soul mates? I didn't peg Erland for the romantic type. But then, I didn't peg him for an astrologer either, yet he is. "So after this girl dumped you, how long before you met Mom?"

"About thirty years."

"Thirty years!" I know Erland's old, but holy crap, that's a long time. "I don't think I can wait thirty years to meet someone else."

"I met other women in that time. But for true love, yes, I had to wait thirty years. I doubt it will take that long for you."

I hope not!

For the first time, I go to my website to find help for *me*.

After chatting with Erland a little more, I head upstairs and log on to oracleofdating.com. It's a great-looking site, colorful and user friendly, thanks to Tracey's web design skills. These days I give most of my advice via live chats. I still have the phone line, but it's barely profitable.

I recall blogging a few times on the topic of breakups. Searching the archives, I find three blogs. *Relationship SOS: Are You about to Break Up?* Obviously it's a little late for that one. *Why a Breakup Can Be Good for You.* I'm not ready to look at the bright side just yet. *Ten Ways to Deal with a Breakup.* Okay, this is the one.

Ten Ways to Deal with a Breakup

1. Cry——get the emotions out. You'll feel better afterward.

2. Write in a journal. Putting your thoughts and feelings into words is a healthy way to work through them.

3. Exercise. If you're anything like me, getting your butt to the gym or out for a run is hard. But afterward you'll feel great. Exercise increases serotonin in the brain, the chemical that makes you feel happy.

4. Listen to boppy, happy music. If you keep listening to sappy ballads, you'll never move on.

5. Get rid of as much evidence of your ex as possible. Take pictures off your wall, move emails from your inbox, put away old letters and gifts. Put them in a box in the back of your closet if you want to look back on them twenty years from now.

6. Make an effort not to hang out at the same places you did with your ex unless, of course, they are your favorite places and you don't want to give them up.

7. Ask your friends not to mention your ex. You don't need to know everything he's doing or who he's doing it with.

8. Open your eyes to the possibilities around you. It's never too soon to appreciate eye candy!

9. Resist the urge to keep rehashing your feelings about the breakup. In the first week or two, vent all you want. After that, keep most of it in or write in your journal. Project the image that you're moving on. Eventually, you'll start to live it.

10. Don't stay home because you feel depressed. Get out and party!

Looks like I'm still at #1, judging by the tears that keep blurring my eyes. It doesn't help that my sinuses are clogged and I can hardly breathe. Breaking up is so not pretty.

My stomach grumbles, and I realize I'd barely gotten through one slice of pizza when Jared dropped the bomb.

I go downstairs in search of comfort food. I think some ice cream is in order.

Why is it people on TV lose their appetite when they're depressed? When I'm depressed, I do nothing but eat. Nestlé's Rollo ice cream, M&M's ice cream and Milky Way ice cream have consolidated two of my favorite vices, ice cream and candy bars. Of course, with my lactose intolerance, too much dairy is never a good thing. So I pop two Lactaid pills and hope for the best.

I head back to my room, bowl of ice cream in hand. Then I notice it on my wall: the painting. Whenever I look at it, my heart swells with love, but now it just deepens my misery. Jared gave it to me one random night, not for any special occasion. It shows a young woman in a field of white blossoms, her hair blowing in the ice-blue wind, a mysterious smile on her face. He said the girl represented me, and the wind was him, madly trying to grasp her hair or her flowing dress, but getting happily caught up in both. I knew that when he gave me the painting, he was telling me he loved me, even though it was a few more weeks before he said the words.

Based on #5 of my own advice, I'd better take down the painting. Should I punch my fist through it, like someone on TV might do? Throw it in the fireplace and dance before the flames while doing a cleansing chant? But I can't destroy the painting, I know that. It reminds me of what a talented artist Jared is and why he deserved that art scholarship. And it's proof that the love between us had been real. To destroy it would be like saying that the love never existed.

I take the painting down and put it in my closet, facing the back wall. Then, since my closet is messy anyway, I throw a cardigan over it so I won't have to see it.

A bleep comes from my computer. It's an instant message for

the Oracle. Forget it. I'm not in the mood to answer questions.
Right now I'm having trouble dealing with my own life.

I try to turn my mind to other things, but then my con-
science kicks in. What if it's important? What if someone
really needs me?

Oracle: Good evening.

NYCgirl224: Hi, Oracle. My family hates my boyfriend. They're
doing everything they can to make me break up
with him. They won't tell me when he calls or
stops by. It's to the point that I have to meet
him in secret.

**Oracle: That must be really difficult for you. Have you
talked to your family about why they feel this
way?**

NYCgirl224: Of course. They think we fight too much. But
all couples fight, don't they? It's normal.
They just don't know him like I do. They don't
see how sweet and loving he is.

**Oracle: Maybe your family's concerned you're not happy with
him.**

NYCgirl224: They're so judgmental. Yeah, he's made some
mistakes, but he's always apologized for them.
He's not a bad guy.

Oracle: What type of mistakes do you mean?

NYCgirl224: Our fights have gotten physical a few times. My
BF's got a bad temper——it runs in his family.

Oracle: Has he hit you?

NYCgirl224: Yeah, but it doesn't happen often. Just when
I make him really angry. And my family judges
him on that, like he's beating me up every day
or something. You can't blame him. He had a
really screwed-up childhood.

Oracle: It sounds like your family is afraid for you. Do you think it's okay that he sometimes hits you?

NYCgirl224: No. I'm not stupid. But sometimes he can't help it. He's working on his anger issues. He says he's going to get counseling.

Oracle: It's not your job to stick by him while he gets help. It's not acceptable for him to hit you—not even once. Let him work out his own problems.

NYCgirl224: *Groan* You sound like my parents. Are you really a teen?

Oracle: I am. But I strongly feel that anyone who hits you has lost his right to be your BF.

NYCgirl224: You just don't understand, Oracle. No one does.

She disconnects. It's the first time a client has ever hung up on me. Did she really think I would support her in staying with her boyfriend? Usually I try to be diplomatic, but I couldn't this time.

Talk about perspective on my situation. A breakup isn't so bad compared with having an abusive boyfriend.

I hope I'll hear from her again, but I doubt it. I can only hope she comes to her senses before it's too late.

That night, as I lie in bed, I can't stop thinking about it: the moment I fell in love with Jared. The moment I knew that my feelings weren't just a trick of teenage hormones, but the real thing.

It was back in January. The school day had just ended, and Jared and I were getting our stuff from our lockers when we saw a crowd gathering in the hallway. We went over to see what was going on, and saw idiot jock Declan McCall giving Evgeney Vraslov a wedgie as a bunch of people cheered him on. Evgeney's glasses had skidded off on the floor, and his face was bright red with humiliation.

Jared dropped his book bag, strode up to Declan and grabbed the collar of his shirt, hoisting him backward. Evgeney dropped to the floor, and Declan stumbled. A hush came over the crowd. No one could believe that someone would dare challenge Declan.

"What the hell?" Declan glared at Jared, rubbing his neck where his collar had bit into it.

"You promised *me* a wedgie, *Dec*."

Now no one, I mean *no one,* called Declan "Dec," apparently due to his dislike of being compared to patio furniture. Since Declan was a little slow, it took him a few seconds to realize that now *he* was the one who looked like a jackass in front of everyone.

Declan got up in Jared's face. I felt my heart pumping with fear. He was big and brawny and had made mincemeat of plenty of guys on the football field. A ripple of excitement went through the crowd as everyone braced for Declan to throw a punch. Several guys started chanting, "Fight!"

Jared held his ground. Didn't even flinch. I realized that although Declan was the bigger guy, Jared had something far more dangerous. He had a quiet, deadly confidence about him. A *please take a shot at me because I'm just dying to hand you your ass* look in his eye that made Declan stop in his tracks.

After a few tense moments, Declan turned and walked away. The crowd, revved up for a fight, erupted in boos.

If ever there was a romantic hero, it was Jared at that moment. He was a guy who'd known trouble in the past—had even been in juvie—and wanted nothing more than to avoid it now. But he'd put himself on the line for Evgeney.

How could I not have fallen in love with him?

two

Sunday night is *Glamour Girl* night for me and my friends. It's our favorite show about rich, spoiled teens and their world of brand names, booze and love triangles. As usual, we're in Viv's basement in Park Slope. Some might think we're a strange mix because we're all so different. Viv, who's from a strict Indian home, is an honors student. Amy is a blonde bombshell who's always looking for a party. Ryan is a metrosexual—a guy who isn't afraid to add frosty blond tips to his hair and doesn't mind being compared to Ryan Seacrest. Sharese is a church-going debate-club member who's never shy about sharing her opinion. As for me, I'm not sure, but I think I'm the one in the middle who brings their different personalities together. I'm also the Oracle of Dating, of course, but Viv is the only one who knows that (and I'd like to keep it that way).

I break the news. There's dead silence for two seconds. Then…

Viv: "That jerk!"

Ryan: "Good-for-nothing ass clown!"

Sharese: "May all his Jonas Brothers hair fall out!"

Amy: "You're way better-looking than him anyway."

At that, I'm slightly comforted, even though I know it's not true.

"We always thought he was weird," Sharese says.

"You did?"

They all nod.

"He was too quiet," Viv says. "It was kind of creepy sometimes."

"He didn't know how to dress," Ryan points out.

I'm surprised by their reaction. I thought they liked Jared. "If you guys didn't like him, you should've told me."

"It's not that we didn't like him," Sharese says. "We just thought he was weird."

"No offense, Kayla," Ryan says, "but you weren't much fun when you were with him. You never went to parties."

He's right about that. Jared preferred that we spend time on our own, and I was happy to just hang out with him. I have to admit, parties mostly lost their appeal because I already had a guy and didn't need to meet one.

"You'll find someone else—don't worry." Amy smiles. "Maybe a guy on the soccer team?" Amy's boyfriend, Chad, is on the soccer team, and Amy is a huge fan of the team's, um, man power.

Viv turns to Amy. "Don't pressure her to find another guy right away. She needs time to discover herself again."

"Self-love, huh?" Amy smiles wickedly.

Viv's eyes flash. "You're such a perv!"

I laugh. I'm glad I have my friends. Too many girls make the mistake of drifting apart from their friends when they're in a relationship—a mistake the Oracle always warns people against. Thank goodness I followed my own advice. I need my friends so much right now.

"What you deserve is a hot stone massage," Ryan says. "Total pampering, total relaxation."

"I can't afford that, but I'll do a mani and pedi."

Ryan looks skeptical. "That's all you ever do. You need to work more shifts at the Hole and save some money."

The Hole, short for Hellhole, is Eddie's Grocery, where Ryan and I work. I have three four-hour shifts a week and that's enough for me. My greatest dream is to make enough money as the Oracle of Dating to be able to quit.

"No spa day is worth more time at Eddie's." I pick up the remote control.

Amy grabs it from me. "No, wait! *Glamour Girl* doesn't start for five minutes and we need to hear more about the breakup. How did he do it?"

"What do you mean, *how?* He just did it. Over pizza."

"Did he at least wait until you were finished eating?" Ryan asks.

"No. I was still on my first slice. But I forgot to leave money, so I guess he paid."

"Damn straight, he should pay!" Sharese says.

"So how did he say it?" Amy asks.

"He said he needed to take a step back and figure stuff out."

They all wince as if they've popped sour candies into their mouths. What Jared said was cliché and we all know it. Taking a step back is the same as needing space or a time-out. It's almost as bad as "we've become different people." Lots of my clients have had those lines thrown at them and the cliché seems to add to the insult. But then, what's a guy to say? *I'm not attracted to you anymore? You bore me?*

"Was that it?" Viv asks. "Is that his only reason?"

"He's really disappointed about not getting an art scholarship. He somehow blames it on being too into me and not focusing enough on his goals."

"Maybe he's trying to punish himself by breaking up with you," Viv offers.

"Too into you?" Sharese says. "What crap."

The others agree that it was a lame thing to say. The stupid part of it was, I believed him. But I guess he was just trying to save my pride. Maybe he thought it was kinder to tell me he'd been too into me than not into me enough.

It doesn't help when Ryan says, "I'm sorry to say this, but he probably met another girl."

Sharese elbows him. "Nice job upsetting her."

"Ouch!" He rubs his ribs. "Well, it's true. It's better if we prepare her for it."

"I believe him that there's no one else, but there could be another girl soon, I know that." Or would there? If he said he needs to take a step back, wouldn't that apply to all girls? Maybe not. If I believe that, I'll be deluding myself.

"You can find someone, too," Amy says. "A rebound can be a beautiful thing."

The red numbers on the clock read 12:27 a.m., but I'm nowhere near sleep. I can think of nothing but rebounding.

REbounding.

ReBOUNDING.

I get out of bed and switch my desk light and computer on. I look up rebounding on an online dictionary.

> 1: To spring or bounce back after hitting something.
> 2: To recover from a disappointment.

The first definition is a lot more fun. I don't want to "recover"; I want to bounce back. Jared is the wall I'm bouncing off. I'm going to bounce off, do a back flip and land in the arms of a cute guy.

I'm aware of what's happening to me. It's textbook for

someone who's been dumped. A void has opened up in my life and I am looking for the quickest way to fill it: what better way than with another guy? Textbook or not, there's nothing wrong with it. It's not like I'm going to fill it with drugs or alcohol.

Come to think of it, I wrote something on rebounding a while ago. I search my archives, and find a blog from last November.

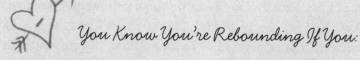

You Know You're Rebounding If You:

★ are too embarrassed to tell your friends you're dating someone new because they'll say it's too soon.

★ believe that dating someone else will prevent you from thinking about your ex.

★ keep thinking of how your ex would feel if he spotted you with your new date (in fact, you hope he will).

The Rebound Equation:

Calculate the number of days you were together and divide it by 8.

Add 30 days if you are the dumpee.

Subtract 20 days if you are the dumper.

Add 30 days if you fantasize about getting back together.

Subtract 20 days if you believe the breakup is for the best, even if you were the one dumped.

= ____ days before you should enter into another relationship.

I grab a calculator. Jared and I were together for five months, three weeks and two days, for a total of 173 days. 173 divided by 8 is 22. He dumped me, so I add 30 days. I add another 30 days because, damn it, I have fantasized about getting back together. Do I believe it's for the best? No!

Total number of days before I can start dating someone else: 82. No way!

Maybe I should reconsider my answers. Did he really dump me? Undoubtedly. Do I fantasize about getting back together? Yes. Is it for the best? Ha! That's where I put the wrong answer. If Jared wanted to break up then, of course, it's for the best. It can't be anything *but* for the best. I should have answered yes.

I subtract 20, which leaves my total at 62 days.

62 days—that's two months! That means I won't be able to date anyone until the middle of May. What was I thinking when I made up the equation? I'm sixteen; I don't have two months to waste!

Of course, I don't *have to* take my own advice.

By the time I get to school on Monday, the breakup is headline news.

Midwood High School is where Brooklyn gamer kids, gangster kids, emo kids and normal kids (me and my friends) collide in a maze of gray hallways. You can hear a dozen different languages in the cafeteria on any given day, not to mention the fact that we have tons of clubs representing diverse nationalities, religions, interests and sexual orientations.

Everybody is tormenting me with questions about the breakup. I can't tell everyone the truth, can I? Thankfully, my friends have already put out the official version of events, and I stick to the story. The official version: Jared and I mutually parted because we've been drifting apart and (Amy added this part) I wanted to see other people.

I know that Jared won't contradict it. He isn't the type to make me look bad. This is the same guy who briefly dated the most popular girl in school, Brooke Crossley, and tricked her into dumping him so he wouldn't have to hurt her feelings.

Speaking of Brooke, she tracks me down in the hallway after first period and plies me with questions—like she has a right to know! Why does she care anyway? She's back with the king of the jocks, Declan McCall.

"So what really happened?" Brooke demands.

"What do you mean?"

"With you and Jared. Come on, you dumped him, right?"

"Ah…it was pretty mutual."

"Was he an asshole to you?" She has the nerve to put an arm around me. Puh-lease. We've never been anywhere close to friends.

"He wasn't an asshole to me."

"Were you an asshole to him?"

"No."

She grimaces. Obviously this isn't as cut-and-dried as she'd hoped. "Then why'd you break up?"

"We grew apart."

"Grew apart? So you don't think, like, he's a total loser?"

"No. I've got nothing bad to say about him."

She looks crestfallen. I'm almost sorry I can't give her a better story. Then she tosses her hair and walks off.

It would have been the perfect opportunity to get revenge on Jared, but I just couldn't do it. If he starts trash-talking me, then I suppose I should do the same to him. But that's not

Jared. And that's not me either. I admit that part of me would love to hurt him the way he's hurt me, but I can't. Sure, I could start some drama, but there wouldn't be a point. I can't break his heart if he's not still in love with me.

At least the official version leaves my ego intact. It makes it seem like I was restless, like I'd had enough of one guy. But the truth is, sticking with one person suits me. When I was with Jared, I didn't want to be with anyone else.

I see Jared a few times in the hallway. We say hi, but neither of us stops walking. It's up to him to stop, since he's the one who did the dumping. If I stop, I'll just seem desperate. Why can't he ask how I'm doing?

His eyes—God, they're bluer than ever—aren't warm. They're not cold either. I'd say they're careful. Maybe they're even a little angry. My friends, I admit, haven't been mature about this. They give him dirty looks or turn away. Even Viv, who's one of the kindest people on the planet, glares at him. I've told them to be nice, but they don't listen. He hurt me, and they believe he deserves to be hurt, too.

In American history class, I can't concentrate. I keep asking myself what I did wrong. I'll make a list...

Top Eight Reasons Jared Got Annoyed with Me

1. I play my favorite songs over and over. Which wouldn't be so bad except:

2. I have no taste in music to begin with (in his opinion). I see nothing wrong with pop music, but he seems to think it's an evil invention meant to enslave the human race.

3. I'm indecisive. Pizza or Chinese is a decision, for example, that takes many minutes of contemplation and perhaps a pros and cons list.

4. He says I don't know how to stop and smell the roses, and that I'm always walking too fast and talking too fast and doing too much.

5. I have been known to complain, especially when I have a bad shift at Eddie's (which, I admit, is practically every shift).

6. People-watching, for me, can be an afternoon's entertainment. I can set up shop at the mall and observe them for hours. For Jared, it's a dead bore.

7. When he gives an opinion, I get upset if it's not what I want to hear. I take things too personally. I take any bit of criticism to heart.

8. I'm a little too focused on *Glamour Girl*. Yes, I have visited the *Glamour Girl* message boards a time or two. Is that a crime?

I read over my list. As far as I can tell, none of those reasons justify breaking up with me.

Another possibility comes to mind. Was I too clingy? We'd talked pretty much every day. But half the time he'd initiated it, so he can't blame me for that, can he?

I know that what-ifs won't get me anywhere. The cold, hard truth is that if Jared had wanted me to do something differently, he could have asked me. Since he didn't, I can only assume he didn't want to work things out.

In chemistry class, my lab partner is Evgeney Vraslov. Skinny, with curly red hair, he's known to most people at school as "The Bulgarian Supergeek." But most people are callous and unfair—Evgeney's a pretty cool guy if you can decipher his thick accent. And smart as all hell, too. I just know he's going to be the next Bill Gates and his former classmates will be kissing his ass.

I have new respect for Evgeney after seeing him do an awesome dance performance months back at the Halloween dance. And he dresses far better than he used to, thanks to the fashion advice on my website. In fact, Evgeney is one of my most loyal clients. He approaches dating like it's a science and appears to study everything I post with the same rigor he gives a chemistry experiment. Anyway, I like chatting with him, and we've become friends. Whenever he decides to go to the cafeteria for lunch instead of hiding away in the computer lab, he sits with me and my friends.

When I drop my books beside him, he says, "I am sorry for your loss." Which is what you'd say if someone died, not after a breakup. But the weird thing is, it touches a chord, and I have to bite my lip to keep it from trembling.

"Thanks, Evgeney. It's for the best."

He looks puzzled. "Why?"

"I don't know. It just is."

I admit, I'd gushed about Jared. Evgeney had asked me about our relationship and I was all too happy to tell him. It's no wonder this new turn of events doesn't make sense to him.

I should come clean. Since he's all about studying relationships, I owe him the truth about mine. Evgeney's faced a lot of rejection himself; he faces it in the hallways of our school every day because he's different. There's no need to put up a facade in front of him.

"Actually," I say quietly, "it was Jared's decision, not mine. It took me by surprise."

He gives a sad nod. "I'm sorry."

I can tell he means it.

By lunchtime, the breakup is old news. Everything is as it used to be, except that Jared isn't sitting with us. He's on the other side of the caf with Tom Leeson and Said Abdullah, two friends he jams with most Thursday nights. Jared doesn't look my way, not even once. I'm so miserable that my stomach feels queasy. How can he ignore me like that?

It's as if the past six months have been erased and Jared is now a stranger. The guy who claimed he couldn't get enough of me has had enough. The guy who could hardly be near me without touching me in some way—entwining his fingers with mine, squeezing my waist—now can't spare me a glance.

I remember the first time he kissed me. It was after school in the art room. I'd felt a hunger inside him that lit me up, scorching us both, forging our connection. Over the next months his kiss had become familiar to me, but the fire had always been there. The hunger for each other. And for me, at least, our connection had only grown stronger over time.

Looking over at him, I see him tipping his head back to drink some soda. Even the act of drinking is somehow sensual, and a rush of longing goes through me. It occurs to me that I should be glad I never slept with him. I'd been sure that he would be my first, but I'd never quite felt ready, and Jared didn't pressure me.

"I can't believe he's just sitting there." Ryan's voice jars me from my thoughts. He's got the evil eye focused squarely on Jared.

Amy snorts. "I think he wore that outfit two days in a row."

I want to rise to Jared's defense. He's still in the foster-care system, living with an elderly Italian lady who sells lingerie to transvestites. He's been saving all of his money for art school, and doesn't have money for new clothes. Plus, I think he has two of the same band shirt.

"Guys, you don't need to talk about him like that. It doesn't make me feel any better."

Ryan turns to me. "It makes *us* feel better."

Viv nods. "At least we know what kind of guy he is. Instead of working through a rough spot, he takes off. I heard about guys like that on *Oprah*."

"Can we please change the topic?" I ask.

"I've got a new topic." Amy looks at Sharese. "Are you going to tell them, or should I?"

"Tell them what?"

"About your new guy, of course!"

"He's not my new guy," Sharese says, shifting in her seat. "We're going out for dinner, that's all."

"Which is obviously a date. Aren't you going to tell them he's an Olympic athlete?"

Sharese rolls her eyes. "It wasn't the real Olympics, I told you. It was the World Transplant Games. Zink's had a bad heart all his life and got a transplant two years ago. He's doing well, but he still needs drugs to make sure his body doesn't reject it."

"Back up a minute," Ryan says. "Did you say his name was Zinc, like the vitamin?"

"It's a mineral," Sharese corrects, "but yes, that's his name. It's his mom's maiden name. It's spelled with a *k* on the end."

Ryan laughs. "What a name! Like he doesn't have enough strikes against him already. So how'd you meet him?"

"He's been in my church youth group on and off for a few years."

I'm glad to hear that Sharese has a new guy in her life. Her last crush, on an ice-cream scooper named Mike P., came to nothing. By the time she'd worked up the courage to give him her number, he'd quit the Dairy Freez, never to be seen again.

"That's so romantic," Viv says. "He struggles with his health for years, and now he can finally ask out the girl of his dreams."

Sharese makes a face. "Easy, turbo. It's only a date."

"So is he cute or what?" Amy asks.

"He's cute, yeah. He's kind of short. His heart condition stunted his growth."

"It's gonna be a hot date, I just know it." Amy gives a sly grin. "I bet he wants to test out his new heart by getting some action."

three

With Regard to Key Lime Pie

When someone finds a partner, we're happy for them. We're so happy we have parties: engagement parties, wedding showers, weddings, gift-opening parties, anniversary parties.

Kaitlin used to have her boyfriend over every Sunday for dinner with her family. They used special plates and there was always a special dessert. Kaitlin's favorite was key lime pie.

But since Kaitlin and her boyfriend broke up, this Sunday dinner ritual no longer applies. No fancy china, no special dessert. There is no denying that, because Kaitlin does not have a boyfriend, her parents do not believe Sundays are worth the extra effort.

Every Sunday, Kaitlin hopes against hope that her parents will buy dessert. She has compassion for her mom, who is watching her waistline, but she still feels that dessert would be nice.

Every Sunday, like clockwork, Kaitlin asks, "What's for dessert?"

The answer is usually "Well, we have some cookies in the cupboard," i.e. nothing.

Where is my key lime pie? she wonders. Don't girls without boyfriends deserve dessert, too?

The Oracle believes there should be a new trend. Let's pull out all the stops to celebrate people who have refused to settle or have been dumped or just like to be on their own. Let's celebrate people who aren't afraid of being single.

Let's serve them key lime pie!

The Oracle of Dating

When you're involved in a breakup, you get every cliché in the book thrown at you. Like when Viv says, "It's better to have loved and lost than never to have loved at all." Ugh. In Viv's defense, she knows about love and loss. Last fall Viv briefly dated Max McIver only to have to break up with him when her parents found out. It was devastating for both of them, but somehow they managed to salvage a friendship. And there's obviously something still between them; they just can't act on it.

Viv's cliché doesn't work for me. Sure, I had a great few months with Jared. I discovered real passion, real companionship. There was nothing I couldn't tell him. I enjoyed the routine of a solid relationship: the daily phone conversations, the lazy days chilling and making out, the messages on my voice mail telling me he missed me.

But is it better to have loved and lost? I don't think so. I was happy with Jared, but that happiness doesn't make up for the pain I feel now. By dumping me, he's taught me a lesson I didn't want to learn—that you can show someone who you really are, you can love them completely, and then without warning, they can turn away from you.

And a breakup isn't just a parting of two people. It's a series of mini-breakups that occur when the primary couple parts ways. You're breaking up with his family and friends, and he's breaking up with yours.

I miss Gina, his foster mom. I miss the way she pinched my cheeks and plied me with cannoli. Will I ever see her again? I can't picture calling her up to say hi. But it seems so strange to have spent so much time with her over the past few months and never see her again. I wonder if Jared will miss Mom and Erland. He got along great with them.

I'm tempted to put some of my thoughts in a blog, but how can I? Jared could surf by and see my innermost feelings spilled onto the page. The last thing I need is for him to know how heartbroken I am. I'd prefer to hang on to what pride I have left.

I admit I've occasionally surfed by his Facebook page and his band's MySpace page. I can't help it, even though I know it's totally unhealthy. What happens when I see that he's chatting with a new girl? Or what if his band posts a new song called "Swinging Single" or something like that? There's too much potential for more pain. So, in a moment of strength, I delete him as my Facebook friend. This way, I won't be able to see his page and I can stop wasting my time.

Another thing about breakups? They're hard because your whole routine changes. Now, after almost six months of a relationship routine, I have huge gaps in my schedule.

With all this time on my hands, I have to ask myself: what did I do with my spare time before I met Jared?

The answer is simple: I used to focus more on being the Oracle of Dating and less on my own love life (or lack of it). When Jared and I got together, I became less focused on expanding my business and only did what was necessary to maintain it.

While I was with Jared, I wrote a blog about every two weeks. Before we started dating, I wrote at least one blog a week, sometimes two or three.

What's up with that? Was I the type of girl to forget her ambition because of a boyfriend?

Well, no more.

I call Tracey, but get her voice mail, and then I remember that she's at her belly dancing class. I decide to call the only one of my friends who knows that I'm the Oracle: Viv.

I explain the situation to her, and she says, "Yeah, I noticed you weren't blogging as much."

Great! I've been letting down my readers. "You should've said something."

"You seemed happy. And busy. I didn't want to pressure you to blog more."

"I let my relationship with Jared sidetrack me. I always thought that I'd be able to quit working at Eddie's by now and focus on the Oracle, but obviously I haven't gotten my butt in gear. I've got to think of how to expand. I need a new business plan."

"Did you have an old business plan?"

"No. Maybe that was the problem. A business should grow over time, shouldn't it? I'm not making any more money than I did six months ago."

"That's because you haven't done anything to broaden your audience. If you want to expand, you have to put the word out. A few flyers at local schools and shopping malls isn't enough."

"But I don't have lots of money to do an advertising blitz."

"You do have *some* money, right? Try investing it in yourself. That's what all entrepreneurs do."

I consider that. I have a few hundred in the bank, since

the Oracle's been in the black for a while. Maybe that money should be invested in advertising. But how can I be sure it'll be worth it?

"I could try buying some advertising space on a couple of teen websites if I can afford it."

"Good idea. Your business is on the web, so web advertising is your best bet."

"Okay. I'll do some research on where would be best."

When we hang up, I surf some websites and contact a few to ask about advertising prices. I have no idea how much advertising costs, but I have the feeling I can't afford most of the sites I'd like to advertise on.

If it takes thousands of dollars in advertising to grow a business, then I don't have a chance. It seems unfair that it takes money to make money.

I've got it! What if I find some popular teen blogs and see if I can do a guest blog for them? That's a way of putting the word out without paying anything. True, most teen bloggers don't have an audience of thousands. But if I can find some who are read by, say, one or two hundred people, that could be useful. What have I got to lose?

My thoughts are interrupted by an instant message.

Cheerlead4ever: I need help, Oracle of Dating. I'm going nuts.

Oracle: What is it, Cheerleader?

Cheerlead4ever: I think my boyfriend is cheating.

Oracle: What makes you think that?

Cheerlead4ever: He spends a lot of time with his guy friends and doesn't always answer my calls. The guys could be covering for him.

Oracle: It sounds like you don't trust him. Why is that?

Cheerlead4ever: He's cheated before. It was the most humiliating thing that ever happened to me, and I can't go through it again. He promised he'll never do it again but how can I trust him?

This is a touchy question. I have a theory about cheaters. If they do it once, they don't have the moral foundation to stop themselves from doing it again.

Oracle: The past can't be changed. If you're sure that you want to give him another chance, then you have no choice but to rebuild the trust that was lost. Otherwise, you'll just be torturing yourself.

Cheerlead4ever: He's not helping any. He thinks I call and text him too much.

Oracle: That's too bad. If he wants to rebuild your trust, he should accept that you'll be suspicious of him, at least for a while.

Cheerlead4ever: I don't think he's concerned about rebuilding my trust. He just expects me to trust him, just like that!

Oracle: He doesn't sound very mature.

Cheerlead4ever: You're right about that!

Oracle: Then the Oracle must ask you: why do you feel you have to be with him?

Cheerlead4ever: Everybody knows we belong together. Even he knows it.

Oracle: Why do you belong with a guy who's cheated on you? Don't you deserve better?

Cheerlead4ever: Of course I do. I'm just waiting for him to figure that out.

Oracle: If this guy is immature, it could be a long time before he figures it out. Or he may never figure it out. Are you willing to put your happiness in his hands?

Cheerlead4ever: Yes, Oracle, I am. Now, can you tell me ways to figure out if he's cheating on me or not?

This girl really doesn't get it. I give her some tips, and by the end of the chat, she seems satisfied that she got what she came for. Once we disconnect, I sit there for a few moments, wondering how anyone can be so obsessed with keeping a cheating boyfriend. The more she told me about him, the scuzzier he seemed. Yet for her, breaking up was not an option.

Far better be single than in a relationship where there isn't trust.

I trusted Jared completely. Until he broke my heart.

Haven't Been Single for a While? Give It a Try!

Now I admit it—the Oracle of Dating is as guilty as anyone of extolling the merits of being in a relationship. I mean, it's the Oracle of Dating, not the Oracle of Singledom. Nevertheless, the Oracle believes that being single is not only a healthy place to be, it's essential for a person's growth. It's a state not to be reviled, but appreciated. And the fact is, being single is downright fun.

Yes, fun. Because being single puts you in a realm where the familiar is replaced by mystery. Who knows who you'll meet at the party Friday night? Who knows what new guy will show up at your school?

So whether you decide it's time to break up with your boyfriend, or whether he's made the decision for you, don't despair. There are infinite romantic possibilities awaiting you…and if you need any help, the Oracle of Dating is always here. ☺

I post the blog with a satisfied nod. I can't believe I haven't written more blogs about being single in the past. I've spent most of my postpubescent life single so I should know a lot about it. I'll have to write more about the joys of singledom in the coming days. And if Jared surfs by the website, all the better—he'll figure I'm happy without him.

"You'll have to free up your schedule next week," Mom says at the dinner table as she's twirling spaghetti around her fork.

"Why?" All sorts of unpleasant possibilities run through my brain. Pie-making with the church ladies? Teen Bible study? Sunday-school nursery duty?

"We have a French exchange student coming," Mom says, too cheerful to be trusted.

"Please tell me you're kidding."

"Mrs. Martin called from the school. They've been having a hard time finding homes for the exchange students. I thought it would be nice if we helped out." She gives an innocent smile, but I know this must be part of some devious plan. For a holy woman, Mom can be downright wicked.

I look to the Swede for help, but his expression is annoyingly cheerful.

"How could you do this without asking me? You know I've been down lately. I don't want to have to show some French girl around." I could see it now: hours in gray museums, endless lineups for tourist attractions. "How long will she be here for anyway?"

"Two weeks." Mom dabs the side of her mouth with a napkin. "And it's not a girl. His name is Benoit and he's seventeen. We thought you'd be okay with that." She and Erland exchange a look.

"Are you serious? You're letting some strange French guy in the house for two weeks! What if he tries to assault me?"

I can tell Mom and Erland are trying not to laugh. Okay, fine, I'm being a bit of a drama queen, but still. A French guy in our house? There's no telling what sort of European debauchery could happen.

"I'll ask him not to assault you, dear," she says. "We don't know for a fact that he's strange. Anyway, I think it will be good for you."

"I have to entertain him for two whole weeks! That's just cruel."

"You won't have to be with him every day, honey. His teachers will have plenty of activities planned. But it would be nice if you took him out a few times."

"You have not been going out much lately," Erland points out. "Now is your chance. Show Benoit the city. You would be great at that. We will give you money toward it."

Mom smiles. "Don't you think it's about time you had some fun?"

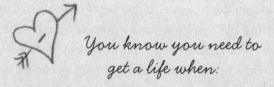

You know you need to get a life when:

★ You check your email dozens of times a day, hoping to hear from your ex-boyfriend—the same ex-boyfriend who hasn't said more than two words to you since you broke up.

★ Your parents have to fly you in a companion from overseas.

★ Your mom buys you a bunch of teen romance novels when she used to tell you to go to the library instead.

★ Your stepdad looks up your horoscope without you even asking him, and says you will find new romance soon. (C'mon, Erland!)

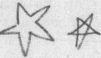

I don't have time to wallow in self-pity, though, because a situation arises that demands my attention. I'm on the phone with my older sister, Tracey, when she says, "Guess what? I'm going to try online dating! I signed up on Lavalife and Match.com."

Uh–oh, this is not my area of expertise. When I think of online dating, I think of freaks, perverts, stalkers.

A little background on Tracey: she's amazing. Really, she's the best sister ever, and she actually likes having me as a little sister. Problem is, she's had bad luck with guys since…well, forever. Tracey hasn't dated much in the past few months. Around the time I got together with Jared, she had a relationship relapse with her ex. After that, she took a few months off dating, but has emerged again, slowly and cautiously. I was intent on setting her up with Jared's gorgeous and spiritual social worker, Rodrigo, but as soon as Tracey decided she was ready to date again, it turned out Rodrigo had a new girlfriend. Talk about timing.

And now this. Internet dating. How can I give her advice when I know so little about it?

"Kayla? Are you there?"

"Uh…yeah."

"Corinne met the sweetest guy online last month. She's talked me into signing up."

"Cool, but you've got to give me a minute to wrap my mind around this. The whole idea scares me. You hear about women getting stalked by people they've met online."

"They get stalked by people they meet other places, too. But you're right, I'll have to be careful. It's still worth exploring. I've known a bunch of people who've met their mates online. Mark at work met his wife through a site years ago, and that was in the early days of online dating. Now there are thousands of potential guys. Mom says that at least half of the couples in her marriage prep courses meet that way."

"Maybe I should try it, too." The word *rebound* flashes in my mind with neon lights.

"Don't you dare. You're too young. And there's no need. When you're in high school and college, there are loads of opportunities to meet guys. It's afterward that things dry up."

"Don't worry, Trace. I'm not going to look for a guy online. But you're right that it's worth a shot for you. Let me do a little research before you go on any dates, okay?"

"Yay! But hurry—I've already started chatting with a couple of guys, and it's only a matter of time before we go out."

Talk about a fire under my butt!

Over the next couple of days, I plunge into the world of online dating. I spend hours surfing the internet for articles, and I check out a bunch of dating websites.

In the end, I come up with:

The Dos and Don'ts of Online Dating

The Dos:

★ Do put up a realistic photo. Sure, replacing your picture with a supermodel will get a guy's attention, but do you really want to see the disappointment in his eyes when he sees the real you?

★ Do look good—but don't go over the top. If you dress up too fancy or wear too much makeup, he may wonder why you're putting so much effort in.

★ Do trust your instincts. If you get a bad vibe from him, then don't spend much time with him and don't tell him many details about your life.

The Don'ts:

★ Don't give out your phone number or call him until after you've met him, unless you have a block up so he can't see your phone number.

★ Don't meet on a Friday or Saturday night. Those nights are prized, and people generally stay out later, which makes it awkward if it's a bad date and you want to go home early.

★ Don't give him your full name until after he's met your approval. Create a separate email account for guys you meet online.

★ Don't let your date see where you live.

★ Don't get into his car.

There must be more, but that's all I can put together for now. I hope it's enough to save Tracey from potential predators. I email her the blog and post it on my website, and none too soon. It turns out Tracey intends to go on a coffee date on Saturday afternoon with a guy who calls himself "Iced Mocha." I am beside myself with anticipation. I offer to go to the café and keep an eye on things, but she says no, that would make her more nervous.

Too bad, because I'd love to put on a hat and sunglasses and play the spy. On second thought, maybe Mom and Erland were right; I need to get out more.

four

11 Days into Rebound Equation

Wednesday-morning pep rally. I'm sitting with my friends at the back of the gym. Sports teams are strutting in front of us while silly mascots are jumping and clapping, as if we care. We would totally sneak out if the teachers weren't watching the doors. It's not that I hate my school, but I don't feel a major allegiance to it. Which I suppose isn't good, considering I'm on student council.

"You wouldn't believe what my mom did," I say. "It's totally heinous."

"She read your diary!" Sharese says.

"I don't have a diary."

"She caught you sexting!" Amy declares.

"I don't sext. That's your thing."

My friends are poised for the news. When I say the words *exchange student,* they shake their heads in disgust.

"I hope you guys will help me entertain him. You will, right?"

"Him?" Amy's eyebrows go up. "Your mom is awesome."

The wave comes our way and we fling our arms upward. "She's obviously hoping to get you some action."

"Yeah, right! That is so not my mom."

"That is so your mom. She knows you need a man. We all know it."

"Well, I did find it odd that she's letting him sleep in my room." I watch their eyes widen. "I'm kidding!"

"My parents would never allow a guy who's not family to stay at my house," Viv says. "Especially a French guy. Don't they all sleep around over there?"

"You can't generalize like that," Amy says. "You can only generalize that French guys are skinny. But Kayla doesn't mind skinny."

"Maybe I do. It depends on the guy."

I refrain from saying that Jared wasn't skinny, he was all lean muscle. I scan the gym, spotting Jared with a couple of guys and a girl at the other end. The girl is a senior named Chelsea Yang. Pretty. Cheerleader. Debate club.

Oh, my God. Chelsea Yang is moving in! My girl radar is certain of it.

I feel a hand on my arm. It's Viv. She knows what I'm thinking.

So does Ryan. "You've raised his market value, Kayla. Before you, Chelsea never would've been interested. But you've made him an acceptable choice."

"I did?" I am not cool with this. I took a chance on him, and now other girls know that he's boyfriend material? No, thank you.

"I bet Chelsea's been waiting for you to break up this whole time," Amy says.

"But why would she be interested in Jared? Wasn't she dating Michael from student council for ages? Jared isn't her type."

"He wasn't your type either, or so you thought," Sharese says. "Things change."

"I can't believe this." Somehow my relationship with Jared has made him a desirable dating choice.

"She's no you, Kayla," Viv says. "Remember that."

"Thanks." But the bleak future is flashing before my eyes. Jared will get together with Chelsea. She will be less clingy, less melodramatic, and an altogether better girlfriend than I was. They will go to prom together, elope to Vegas, then go off to college and share one of those married couple dorm rooms which I've always thought were so cozy and romantic.

This line of thought is not working for me. "I'm going to the bathroom." I get up quickly before one of my friends can offer to join me.

I hurry there, expecting to burst into tears. But the tears don't come. Sadness seems to be locked in my throat. I'm standing at the sink, looking at myself in the mirror. *How could you do this to me, Jared, when you promised to never hurt me?*

I force myself to breathe in and out until I feel calm again. I finally straighten and leave the bathroom. When I go back into the gym, I refuse to look in Jared's direction. *Rebound,* I tell myself. I've got to move on.

That night I write a blog called *A Viable Option,* discussing the idea that who you're seen dating determines who will consider dating you next. I'm still reeling at the fact that go-getter Chelsea Yang may be going for Jared.

Or was she around the whole time? Were she and Jared secretly friends, just waiting for me to be out of the picture before they became more?

I try to banish the thought. Unless I'm faced with evidence to the contrary, I'm going to believe Jared didn't dump me for another girl.

Still, I have to wonder about what Ryan said—that I somehow raised Jared's stature by dating him for so long. But why? He dated Brooke before me, the most popular girl in school. She's the one who made him a viable option, not me.

Or maybe not. She dumped him, claiming he was a jerk for demanding sex. But the truth was, it was just a ploy to make her break up with him. I suppose Jared might've remained a dating no-no if I hadn't scooped him up after that.

When you think about it, the fact that Jared and I stayed together for six months showed Chelsea and all the other girls at school that Jared was a keeper. And, damn it, we probably looked happy. Because we *were* happy. At least, I thought we were. I still don't know when that changed.

I wish it worked both ways. I wish there was a group of gorgeous, dangerous (but not really) guys waiting for Jared and me to break up so they could ask me out. But no one has, and frankly, that type of guy doesn't seem to exist except in Jared.

Thank God for my business. At least I have something to focus my energies on. I decide that instead of draining my bank account on paid advertising, I'll visit some teen blogs. I contact several popular sites. Within a few days I hear back from most of them, and five say they'd be happy to have me. Four of them ask me to write guest blogs, and the fifth asks me to answer a question submitted by a reader.

I start work on the four blogs. None of them has given me a deadline, but I'd like to put all of them out over the next month. The blogger who asked me to answer a reader's question puts out an open call for questions for the Oracle of Dating. Her website, teenmoi, must be really popular, because I get an extra sixty hits the day she mentions me in her blog.

When Amy tells me about a house party happening on Friday night, I decide it's time to leave the computer and go out for a change. And then I find out that my friends can't go. At least, Ryan and Sharese can't go. Viv isn't interested. She can't see why we'd go to a party when we don't even know Tara Franklin, the senior who's hosting it.

Thankfully, Viv responds to pressure. So I tell her how I really need to get out and how it would be awkward to go with just Amy and Chad, and Viv caves. Booyah!

"You have to introduce Kayla and Viv to your soccer buddies," Amy says to Chad on the subway there.

"No probs." Chad is an easygoing guy with a cute face and soccer bod. He seems happy to leave it to Amy to do all the talking and decision-making. I've never really understood why he and Amy have been together so long—it must be two years by now. I think the passion wore off a while ago. Plus, Amy often flirts with other guys, and sometimes takes it into the realm of cheating. I don't know why she has a boyfriend when she seems to enjoy playing the field so much.

I check my hair and makeup in my compact. I braved the straightening iron—something I don't do lightly—and successfully glammed up my makeup without looking like a showgirl. The hour I spent putting myself together was worth it. I'll be able to walk into the party with confidence.

Tara's house is on a swanky block in Brooklyn Heights. When we get there it's around ten, and the place is pumping. A random kid answers the door. The inside of the house is posh, with mainly black furniture, white walls and expensive-looking artwork. I can't imagine why anyone who lives in such a nice place would have a house party, since the term itself is synonymous with destruction. But that's not my problem.

We're instantly swept into the crowd. I find myself surrounded by beer bottles and people I vaguely know. I'm glad that Viv is by my side because Amy and Chad have gone missing. Rock is blaring from speakers throughout the house, making it difficult for us to hear each other.

Amy and Chad are back, slipping cold beers into our hands. I nod my head to the music. Half a beer later, I'm slipping into a happy mood where nothing can touch me.

Okay, maybe not. I spot Jared's friend Tom in the kitchen with his girlfriend. We say hi, and that's it. But it sucks because Jared's in my head now. I wonder if there's any chance he'll show up tonight. Maybe he will, now that he's newly single. I half hope he will, because I want him to see that I'm out having fun.

Damn it, I don't need to be reminded of Jared when I'm trying my best to have a good time!

I look over at Amy. I've never seen someone so hell-bent on letting loose at parties. I could understand if she were reserved and repressed most of the time, but she's far from it. Right now she and Chad are dancing—well, *she's* dancing, and he's standing above her enjoying the show. In fact, she's dancing in a way that makes certain every guy within a ten-yard radius is noticing her. Chad's catching their looks and trying to stare them down one by one, but it's not enough. It will never be enough. When Amy wants attention, she gets it.

After a while Chad and Amy get tired of dancing and return to us. They come bearing gifts: more beer and Chad's soccer teammates Greg and Sandeep. I don't dare a glance at Viv, but I know we're thinking the same thing: these guys are HOT, and one of them is Indian! That's when our good time goes into high gear.

Beautifully built, with Mario Lopez dimples, Greg is a senior at Madison High School. Although it's hard to hear everything he's saying, I know we're getting along super well. Our body language is hot, too. Greg's hand is propped on the wall behind me, creating an intimate cocoon. Anyone watching would say he's definitely into me.

He leans in, inhaling deeply. "I love that perfume."

"Thanks, it's Happy Heart."

He nuzzles my neck, making an *mmm* sound. I shiver.

"I wasn't expecting to meet anyone tonight," he says.

"Neither was I." Which is true. I was *hoping,* but not expecting.

His lips brush against mine, and we're kissing, slow and hot. A voice in my head, the Oracle's voice, tells me this isn't going to lead to a lasting relationship. But what the hell? I can have some fun.

Out of the corner of my eye, I'm aware that Tom Leeson is walking by. Maybe he'll report this back to Jared. I hope he does. I want Jared to know I'm moving on.

At some point I realize I'm officially drunk. There's no doubt about it because (a) my head is swimming, and (b) I've totally lost track of my friends. Did Viv tell me that she and Sandeep were going to dance? Have Amy and Chad gone to grab a bite to eat? I can't remember.

"You wanna go upstairs?" Greg asks. The sexy dimples float in front of my face.

"Sure, but I'm not going to…you know."

He takes my hand and we go upstairs. Although I'm drunk, I'm not clueless as to what's happening. I know that I'm going to make out with him, but that I'm going to keep my clothes on. I have strictly defined boundaries. Jared always respected that.

We end up in a guest bedroom. It's so classy and neat that I don't want to rumple the duvet, but Greg says we'll straighten it up later. He whips his shirt off and starts kissing me on the bed. I kiss him back. "You're a wildcat," he whispers in my ear. "Let's get naked." He starts tugging at my shirt.

I stiffen. "I just want to, you know, kiss."

"Oh, come on. We could've done that downstairs."

God, this isn't romantic. "I'm keeping my clothes on."

"Fine, whatever you say." He's back to kissing me. I get comfortable again, relaxing beside him.

Then his hand slides into my jeans.

"Whoa." I pull back. "What was that?"

"What? I wasn't taking your clothes off."

"Yeah, but—"

"Come on, just relax, Kate."

I roll away, sitting up. "Kayla."

"Sorry." He grins. "I don't want to pressure you, Kayla."

"Well, that's what you're doing!"

He shakes his head at me. "You're a tease."

"No, I'm not. You're a manipulative predator who preys on vulnerable women!"

"Crazy bitch!" He puts his shirt back on and storms out.

I burst into tears. What the hell was I thinking?

Oh, God. I think I'm going to throw up.

I feel like crap.

I'm so sick and depressed that I stay in bed most of the next day. I can handle the hangover. What I can't handle is the situation I put myself in last night. I trusted a guy I didn't know.

I can't even remember how much I drank. Thank God I'd had enough clarity to tell him to back off. What if I'd been too drunk to stop him? What if I'd passed out? Would he have had sex with me anyway?

Damn it, I've always prided myself on being too smart to get into a situation like that. And yet that one slip almost resulted in disaster.

Stupid, stupid, stupid!

Is this what the breakup with Jared has done to me? Made me into an idiot? Forget that!

I drag myself out of bed and go to the computer. I know what I have to do.

Warning: When You Are Vulnerable, the Vultures Will Move In

I wish I could say that when you are feeling low, the arms of the universe will wrap around you and protect you. But it doesn't always work that way.

The universe offers you the opportunity to pick your direction: healing or self-destruction.

When we are going through difficult times, many of us make big mistakes. Some teens experiment with drugs. Some turn to sex. Some turn to alcohol.

While any of these might give you temporary relief, they will only increase your pain in the long run. In fact, you are likely to end up in a situation far worse than the one you started out in.

When you are vulnerable, you attract predators. People who will try to have sex with you. People who will offer you drugs. People who will help you screw up your life in any number of ways.

So the next time you are feeling low, keep this in mind: it could get worse. Don't let it.

Don't choose self-destruction. You deserve better.

Yours in solidarity,
The Oracle of Dating

A few minutes later, the phone rings.

"Kayla."

"Jared?" It's surreal to hear his voice.

"I need to know what's going on."

"What are you talking about?"

"The party. Your blog. What happened to you?"

"Uh, nothing."

"Not nothing. Tom said you were with some guy at the party last night. Said you went upstairs. Said you were drunk. Now you're writing about predators trying to have sex with you!"

"Who says the blog's about me?"

"C'mon, Kayla. You always write about what you know. It either happened to you or one of your friends."

"Well, okay, it is about me, but the guy backed off."

"But he tried to take advantage of you, did he? What's this guy's name?"

"Why do you want to know?"

"I want to kill him."

I'm shocked. I've never heard Jared talk that way before. "He didn't rape me, Jared. Thanks for caring, I guess. It's weird though. You're calling to find out if I got raped, but you never even called to see how I was doing after we broke up."

There's a long pause. "I hate that I hurt you."

A lump forms in my throat. "I—I have to go." He wants me to tell him that it's okay, but I can't. It would be too big a lie.

Later that night, I reach for one of the books my mom bought me.

It's a small yellow hardcover called *The Prophet,* by Khalil Gibran. It's a story told in poetic language about a prophet who comes to a village to share his wisdom.

Does it make sense that a book can be a comfort? That these words written almost a hundred years ago could be a balm to my soul? I don't know if it makes sense, but it's true. The book is short, and I meditate on every passage before moving on to the next one.

Life. Love. Death. Acceptance. As I'm reading, a new seren-
ity comes. I realize that I did the best I could in my relationship
with Jared. I loved him, and I showed him the truest part of
myself. There is no use focusing on the things I might have
done wrong. I'm human and bound to make mistakes. We
didn't break up because of something I did, or something I
wasn't.

Jared and I were together for almost six months. How much
worse would it have been if we'd been together for two years,
or five? What if we'd married and had kids?

Gradually I'm gaining perspective. This isn't the end of the
world.

One thing is sure—having my heart broken gives me insight
into breakups that I didn't have before. Maybe it'll make me
a more compassionate person.

Maybe it'll help me do a better job as the Oracle of
Dating.

five

15 Days into Rebound Equation

"So…"

"So, what?"

"How'd it go with Sandeep today?" I give Viv a friendly nudge.

Everyone turns to stare at her. *Glamour Girl* starts in ten minutes—just enough time for a recap of Viv's afternoon coffee date with Sandeep, the cute Indian guy from the party.

"He's amazing." Viv's big brown eyes take on a dreamy expression. "We're on the same wavelength about so many things."

"Like what?"

"We're both serious about school. He's got a sense of family loyalty that I really respect. And we've got the same quirky sense of humor. But it's complicated."

"He *is* Indian, right?" Ryan asks. "Then why's it complicated?"

She twists her hands in her lap. "He has a girlfriend."

We all gape at her.

She rushes on, "But he's not happy with her. She's really needy. She hardly has any friends—her life totally revolves around him. So he feels responsible for her."

"Is he going to break up with her?" I ask.

"He wants to, but it's…"

"Let me guess—complicated?" Ryan offers.

"It is. Her sister's wedding is coming up in a month and he doesn't feel he should dump her before then."

We all look at each other, deciding what to think of this.

"It could be a valid reason," Sharese says. "You don't want to shake somebody up before a big family event."

"I think a month is plenty of time for someone to recover from the shock of being dumped." Ryan glances my way. "What do you think?"

Great, I'm the resident dumpee. "Depends on the girl. A month would be fine for me."

"I hate to say it, honey, but the guy's playing you." Amy looks up from the nail she's filing. "Guys don't do anything they don't want to do. If he's staying with her, it's because it's working for him."

Viv is exasperated. "What about compassion? It's like with my uncle. He's stayed with my aunt forever even though she has bad mood swings and treats him horribly. He's worried that she might hurt herself if he leaves."

Amy shrugs. "Your uncle's a saint then. Give him a medal. Sandeep is a teenage guy. They don't operate that way."

"What are you saying? That we guys just think with our crotches?" Ryan asks, getting all huffy and puffy.

"That's exactly what I'm saying."

"You're bang on, baby." He laughs, and the rest of us laugh—except Viv.

"Sandeep's not like that! I know it sounds bad, but if you

talked to him, you'd see what type of guy he is. It's just that his girlfriend is really fragile and dependent so he has to be careful."

"I hate to say it, but there are some red flags here." She knows what I'm saying isn't just a random observation; it's coming from the Oracle of Dating. "Guys who cheat always say they're in unhappy relationships and plan to break up with the girl. They often paint her as pathetic, someone they're staying with out of pity."

"Good point," Sharese says. "And here's another thing I just thought of. Won't he end up in the wedding pictures? He's not doing her any favors if she's going to see him in the pictures forever."

"He probably hasn't thought of that." Viv lifts the remote control. "Show's coming on." She turns up the volume, cutting off the discussion.

Ouch. I can see she's disappointed by our reaction to Sandeep, and maybe even angry that we're not giving him the benefit of the doubt. But I have to question a guy who's going to flirt with a girl at a party and go for coffee with her the next day while he still has a girlfriend. If he's in a messy situation, he should wait until he gets out of it before dragging somebody else in. My instincts say Viv shouldn't trust this guy.

For her sake, I hope I'm wrong.

Now this won't be so bad at all.

He is on the doorstep, a duffel bag slung over one shoulder, a carry-on over the other. He hasn't had the chance to ring the doorbell yet, but I saw the taxi pull up.

"Hi, Benoit. I'm Kayla."

"*Allo.*"

Boy, is he ever tall! He must be six-three at least. He has a thick mop of brown hair and classic, aristocratic features like you see in old movies. His eyes are gray and heavy-lidded. I've read about gray eyes in romance novels but I've never seen them before.

I wish I'd primped for this! How could it not have occurred to me that this guy would be cute? I am way too casual in a loose tee and jeans. My hair is kind of scraggly and I'm not wearing any makeup.

Just as I reach out to shake his hand, he leans forward to kiss my cheek. We laugh awkwardly. "Sorry, I am not used to greeting this way," he says, shaking my hand. "In France, we kiss both cheeks."

"Oh, right, I've seen people do that." I can't believe I just blew my chance to be kissed on both cheeks by a sexy French guy!

I lead him upstairs to Tracey's old bedroom, which is freshly dusted and vacuumed. Too bad the same daffodil wallpaper has been up for more than a decade.

He looks around, and sits down on the bed.

"My parents will be home for dinner in about an hour, in case you were wondering."

He smiles. "I was not wondering."

"Do you want a snack in the meantime? Or maybe a nap or something?"

"I will—" he gestures with his hands "—my stuff."

"Unpack?"

"Yes. I will unpack then I will join you."

I open some dresser drawers to show him they're empty. "I'll make some tea. Do you like tea?"

"I prefer wine." He winks. "But tea will do, Kayla."

Oh, my God, he's flirting with me! Yay!

I hurry downstairs and put the kettle on. Then I go to the fridge, take out the double-cream brie specially bought for the occasion, then cut some triangles and put them on a plate with water crackers.

Benoit comes down twenty minutes later, having changed his shirt, combed his hair and put on cologne. I want to pinch myself that such a cute guy has landed in my kitchen. Or is this too good to be true—an April Fool's joke one day early?

He sees the spread on the table. "Ah, you didn't have to."

"French people like cheese, right?"

"Certainly, we do. We like crisps and junk food, too."

"Crisps?"

"Yes. My English teacher was British. Crisps, you call them chips." He sits down while I pour the tea.

"Milk and sugar?"

"Only milk, thank you."

I sit down across from him. "So are you excited to be in New York?"

"Yes, especially in Brooklyn." I love the way he says *Brook-leen*. His accent is totally a dorable, especially how he pro-nounces *th* like *z*. "It is a strange and scary place in movies, with guns and gangs and such things. But from the taxi it looks like…a normal place."

"You haven't seen all of it yet, trust me."

"You will show me, I hope."

"I'll show you whatever you want, although I know the exchange organizers have a lot of things planned for you." Mom had to reassure me that Benoit wouldn't be my problem 24/7, but now being his tour guide doesn't seem so un-appealing.

"Pff! I do not have to go everywhere with them. I did not come here to be with French peoples."

I grin. "You're a rebel, are you? Won't your parents get mad if they find out that you strayed from the group?"

"Americans have parents like police or something? In France, I have my own car. I drink when I feel like it. Go to clubs. I do whatever I want."

"Don't tell my mom and stepdad that. They'll be afraid you'll corrupt me."

"Corrupt you? I am in America—you are supposed to corrupt me." He smiles, sipping his tea. "Where are you taking me tonight?"

"Tonight? Aren't you supposed to be tired?"

"I will take a coffee after dinner, then I will be fine. I have—what you call it? Adrenaline. I would never sleep."

"Okay, then after dinner we'll go somewhere." My mind whirls. Hmm, what could I show him that doesn't require advance tickets or planning? There's always Times Square. Out of the blue I picture Jared and me walking there on our second date, and I'm not so keen anymore. "How about we go to a funky café in the Village and take a look at some of the shops? Have you heard of the Village?"

"Yes. East or West or Green-witch?"

"You've been reading up on New York, have you?"

"I have the Frommer's guide."

I hear a car door slam. "That's probably my stepdad. Mom promised she'd be home by five-thirty. So we'll have dinner and be out of here by seven. How does that sound?"

He grins. "You are the boss."

Dinner is Mom's meat lasagna, pre-prepared yesterday, crusty baguette and asparagus. For a Wednesday night, it's a real feast and Benoit looks like he's enjoying it. He chats with Mom and Erland, and they seem to like him, though they ask him way too many questions. Apparently he's taken English classes since the first grade. He says that American and British movies are big in France and watching them in English is a matter of principle for young people. Subtitles and dubbing are for the older generation.

When I announce that I'm taking him out after dinner, Mom frowns. "Benoit is probably very tired. Maybe tomorrow you can show him around."

"I slept the whole flight," Benoit says. "I would be happy if Kayla could show me some of your city. There is much to see."

"If you're sure. Try not to be too late." Looks like Mom is falling under Benoit's spell.

After dinner, Benoit goes up to get ready. Mom gives me a nudge. "He's cute, isn't he?"

I know better than to walk into that trap. If I admit that he's cute, she'll tease me constantly. "He's okay, if you like the French look."

Then I go upstairs, change my outfit, brush my hair, my teeth, roll on extra deodorant, put on makeup and grab my purse all in ten minutes flat. I find Benoit waiting at the bottom of the stairs. We're out of the house before Mom and Erland have a chance to see that I made an effort to look good.

We chat the whole way to the subway station, and I walk him through the steps of buying a metro card at the machine. While we're waiting on the underground platform, we look at the big subway map. I show him where we are and where we're going.

"It looks as big as Paris," he says.

"Have you spent much time there—in Paris, I mean?"

"Not much. I come from Aix-en-Provence in the south.

It takes five hours to drive to Paris. I don't like it there. The people are snobs."

I've heard that applies to the French in general, but I don't say so. Obviously it isn't true. Benoit is the only French person I've ever met and he's friendly. Statistically, that's a good sign.

We ride the train to West Fourth Street. I thought the Village would be a good place to take him, since it's a snapshot of funky New York style. When we emerge from the station, the streets are busy with people shopping, strolling and socializing. It's one of those unseasonably warm April evenings that makes you want to be anywhere but indoors.

"A lot of students live in this neighborhood, since NYU is just a few blocks away. I don't know how they can afford it. It's become super expensive around here. See that big shiny building? Mary Kate and Ashley Olsen used to live there."

"I see it, but who are they?"

I grin up at him. "That's refreshing!"

He looks puzzled. "What?"

"Here in America, we have an obsession with celebrities. Have you heard of Brangelina or TomKat?"

"No, I have not. But I saw Johnny Depp in Toulouse."

"Wow!"

We stroll around the Village browsing shops. Benoit is especially interested in a shop called Earth's Treasure, which has imports from Thailand and India. We admire a bunch of stuff: wooden chests, sculptures, notebooks with homemade paper and smocks like the Dalai Lama would wear.

Benoit stops and inhales deeply. "I love the smell of incense, don't you?"

"Uh, sure, yeah." I don't mention that incense reminds me of the bathroom. Mom says it's better than air freshener.

I take him into a store called Frew Frew. He looks around with one eyebrow raised. He glances at a price tag for some frumpy old jeans. "One hundred and fifty dollars for this?"

"You're paying for the designer label. Funny, isn't it? If I were to see somebody in those jeans, I'd have thought they got them at the Salvation Army."

Maybe I spoke a little too loudly, because a pierced and tattooed salesgirl in fishnets looks me up and down as if to say I'm no hotshot myself.

Later we stop at a café. It's crowded with people straining to read books or work on laptops despite the low lighting. I order a decaf soy latte. Benoit gets a café Americano.

It's incredible how I barely know this guy yet we get along so well. Benoit is full of questions, and I'm not talking about "what do you do for fun?" He asks questions about how Americans view the president, the economy, the environment and all that. He sounds more like a sociologist than a high school student. He's smart and sexy rolled up into one gorgeous European package.

At one point the conversation lapses, and I can't for the life of me think of what to say next. I think we've talked about everything humanly possible.

"Un ange passe," he says.

"What does that mean?"

"In France, when the conversation goes quiet, we say an angel passes."

"That's beautiful."

He looks at me. "That is not the only thing that is beautiful."

"Thanks." I can feel myself blushing. "You're pretty good with words."

"What can I say? Words, they are part of *séduction,* are they not?"

"Did you say seduction?"

"Mais, oui."

Oh, my God! Benoit is not a virgin for sure. Sensuality drips from everything he does—even the way he holds his coffee cup! Is he going to sneak into my room tonight and introduce me to the erotic arts?

His eyes glitter with amusement. "You think I mean sex, don't you?"

"Uh..."

"In France, *la séduction* means many things. Mainly, it is to bring someone closer to you. To charm them."

"And you want to charm me?"

"I don't know if it is even possible to charm a...Brookleen girl. But I will try."

"Kayla, are you with us?"

I snap out of my open-eyed doze and sit up straight. "Yes, Ms. Cheney."

A discussion of *Macbeth* is swirling around me. All I can think about is how I caught Benoit leaving the bathroom this morning wearing only a towel. His upper body was pale and well built, his stomach flat. My wonder must have shown on my face because he winked at me.

If we were in a romantic comedy, a puppy would've run by and snatched the edge of the towel, ripping it clean off him. But, of course, I don't have a puppy and Benoit's hold on his towel was annoyingly secure.

If we were on a soap opera, he would have dropped the towel on purpose and, bashful virgin that I am, I would have gotten a good look and then run off, scandalized.

But if we were in one of those late-night French movies, he would have dropped the towel and I would have stood my ground and looked him up and down. But what comes next I'll never know, since I'm terrified to watch anything even slightly erotic because Mom and Erland are always around.

Last night with Benoit was fantastic. We had an instant connection. It felt like we'd known each other for years instead of hours. If it had been a first date, it would have scored off the charts. Maybe that's why it was so great—because it wasn't a date. We were just two people getting to know each other with no strings, no expectations. It was the best non-date ever!

There was nothing we couldn't talk about. He told me all about his family and friends back in Aix-en-Provence (which he calls "Ex") and the freedoms they have there. Drinking and smoking among teens is normal and parents don't have a fit over it. But then, teens don't binge drink like they do here. Because drinking and smoking aren't a big deal over there, teens are less likely to go overboard.

Well, that's the only downside to Benoit—he smokes. But he didn't complain when I told him that, due to city laws, he couldn't smoke inside public buildings. And when I warned him not to smoke at my house, he said he wouldn't have anyway.

He asked about my family and friends, and I told him stories about them, using the funniest anecdotes I could think of. The only person I left out was Jared. Talking about him would only be a downer.

Benoit was particularly fascinated by the fact that my mom is a minister. He said that he and most of his friends reject the Church and everything about it. In fact, he's an atheist. I said that I have respect for most religious and non-religious traditions, as long as they have a basic morality and aren't Satanic or anything. That made him laugh.

I so hope to see him this evening. I don't know when he'll get home because the exchange organizers have a bunch of activities planned. I think today is the Guggenheim Museum. Which I don't understand, because can't they see all that European art back home?

When I get home from school, I waste no time. I freshen up, put on some cutesy around-the-house clothes and wait for Benoit.

Eventually it becomes clear that he's not coming home for dinner. So I eat with Mom and Erland and suffer through their questions about last night. Where did we go? What is he like? Are we getting along?

"He won't be back until late, in case you were wondering," Mom says. "They went to a Broadway show."

"Oh, okay." Couldn't she have told me a couple of hours ago?

After dinner, I head up to my room to do homework. When I'm finished, I put the books aside to become the Oracle again. I answer a couple of standard "does he like me?" questions. I have to gently reply "probably not" to both of them. In most cases, when a girl writes asking if a certain guy likes her, it's because she doesn't want to accept that he doesn't. Just because he occasionally flirts with her doesn't mean he wants to date her. Bottom line: if a guy's interested, he'll let you know.

By ten-thirty fatigue is hitting me hard. I usually don't crawl into bed until eleven, but last night we didn't get in until midnight, and I was so wired it took me a good hour to fall asleep.

I wash up, get into my pj's and turn off the lights. About

fifteen minutes later, I hear the front door open. Benoit is downstairs talking to my mom. Then I hear him walk up the stairs.

He taps lightly on my door. "Kayla?"

"Come in."

He enters. "Sorry, you were sleeping."

I turn on the bedside lamp. "I wasn't asleep. Come in and tell me about your day."

He drops his knapsack and sits on the edge of the bed. "The Guggenheim was interesting. As for the show, it was okay, but I would have preferred to sneak out and meet you somewhere. I couldn't because my teachers were counting our heads like we were babies."

"Lame."

"What is 'lame'?"

"It means totally annoying."

"Then, yes, it is lame. I did not come here to be with them—I would rather be with you. My *professeur* says that if we leave the group, we will be penalized and maybe lose credit for English class. But if we get permission to do something with our host family, that will be all right."

"Then that's what we'll do. We'll tell them you're hanging out with us all the time."

"Yes. You can help me. We can draw up an *itinéraire* of activities. They cannot say no."

"Great! Should we do it now?"

"Tomorrow morning is fine. You must sleep." He gets up. "I look forward to spending time with you, Kayla."

"Me, too." I am tingling all over now. "Good night, Benoit."

"*Bonne nuit, mon chou.*" And he leaves the room.

Though I don't know what *mon chou* means, I'm sure it's a good thing. I fall back onto my pillow with a dazed smile— and the delicious feeling that my love life might be turning around.

six

20 Days into Rebound Equation
(But who really cares? Benoit is here.☺)

The next day, I meet Benoit at four o'clock on Thirty-fourth Street at Sixth Avenue. When he kisses both of my cheeks, my knees tremble. It's incredible, this vibe between us.

We chat about our days as we walk the couple of blocks to the Empire State Building. There's a huge lineup outside.

"Should we bother?" he says.

"It's up to you. I don't mind waiting."

"It doesn't matter." He smiles down at me. "Do you really think we will visit all of the places we told your parents?"

As realization dawns, I smile back at him. From this point on, there will be no itinerary. Benoit doesn't want to *see* New York, he wants to experience it.

"Where should we go from here?" I ask.

He takes my hand. "Let's just walk for now."

As we walk, I glance down at our hands. This is surreal. I wonder if he can feel my pulse pounding through my wrist.

We spend the next hour in the concrete jungle of Midtown.

He stops in front of a huge statue on Fifth Avenue and says he recognizes it from the cover of an Ayn Rand book called *Atlas Shrugged*. He takes a picture, telling me he's going to turn it into a poster for his bedroom wall.

"You're a fan of Ayn Rand?" I ask. I know that she was a writer and there was a movie about her, but that's it.

"I am not a fan of Rand in particular. She was a communist. Interesting, but not for me. Is that a bookstore?"

Benoit's eyes light up, and we head for Barnes and Noble. Usually I go to the fiction, self-improvement or teen sections, but this time I follow him. We end up downstairs in the philosophy section.

I pick up a book called *The History of Sexuality* by Michel Foucault, thinking the Oracle might benefit from it. Benoit shakes his head. "Maybe not what you are looking for. Try this instead." And he finds me a book by Noam Chomsky on human nature.

As I watch him pore over philosophy books, I ask myself if I should tell him about the Oracle. I'm sure I can trust him. And it would be cool to share my secret and hear his thoughts on dating and relationship questions.

"I'll be in the self-improvement section on the second floor," I say.

He looks intrigued, but just nods. He'll understand later.

We spend more than an hour in the bookstore. I buy *The Buddhist Guide to Loving Relationships* written by some bald monk and on sale for $8.99. I figure it's a good buy since I'm on a spiritual, self-help kick these days. As for Benoit, he sees a rack with classics on sale for $3.99 each, so he stocks up: Herodotus, Plato, Aristotle, Aquinas. He says he welcomes the challenge of reading them all in English.

A half hour later, we're sitting in a restaurant on the Lower

East Side—it's not fancy, but the prices are reasonable. It's certainly better than in Midtown where you can pay ten dollars for a small sandwich. I ask Benoit about his ambitions. He wants to be a professor of philosophy at a university, but he says professorships are hard to come by in France. So he may teach philosophy or history at a high school, or switch gears and go into art history and be a curator.

I think about how hot he would look as a curator at the Louvre, and I ask him if he's read *The Da Vinci Code*. He says it has no basis in reality. I say that my mom would agree with him but I still think it's a damned good read.

"What about you, Kayla? What career do you want?"

"I'd like to be a counselor of some kind. Giving relationship advice is my thing. I actually have a website called the Oracle of Dating."

"A website of your own?"

"Yes. People pay me to answer their questions, and I write blogs on relationships."

"That is brilliant! Can I see it?"

"Sure, I'll show you when we get home."

"That explains the books you were looking at. Why are you interested in such things?"

I shrug. "Human relationships seem to follow patterns. I like identifying those patterns and making sense of them. And the feeling you get when you help someone is awesome."

"You are a healer of relationships, and you are named after St. Michael. He was a healer, too." Benoit moves the bottle of ketchup aside and touches my hand. "*Chère* Kayla, you fascinate me, do you know that?"

He's a master of French flirtation. Well, I'd like to think I'm an accomplished flirt myself. I give him a mysterious smile. "The fascination is mutual."

★ ★ ★

Maybe Oprah is right. Maybe the universe does have a plan for everyone.

Is it a coincidence that Benoit came into my life a short time after Jared left it? According to *The Buddhist Guide to Loving Relationships,* there are no coincidences. It's the universe conspiring to help you.

After the near disaster at the house party, I admit, I nearly lost faith in the universe's plan for me. But I'm now changing my mind.

I'm thinking this as I sit at my desk, reading emails for the Oracle. I look over at Benoit, who is lying on my bed reading Herodotus. He's so tall that his legs are dangling off the end.

He catches me watching him and cocks a brow. "Working hard, Oracle of Dating?"

"Always."

Benoit has been here a week now, and hardly a moment goes by that I'm not with him or thinking about him. In the evenings, we explore the city, walking the streets or riding the subway to random places. We've spent hours in cafés and bookstores.

Mom and Erland know that I like him. It's pretty obvious, since I never used to wear mascara, eyeliner and lipgloss around the house. The worst part about them knowing that I'm crushing on the French guy? They *like* it. "It's a little excitement for her," they're probably saying behind my back. "It'll help her get over Jared."

Jared? I've hardly thought of him since Benoit arrived. It's wonderful.

I go over and sit on the corner of the bed. "Enjoying Herodotus?"

"Yes, although he is rather verbose. I prefer Thucydides.

He gets to the point." Benoit puts the book facedown and sits up, looking wistful. "It is so great, being here with you."

"I know what you mean. I certainly didn't expect this." I look away, feeling a little shy.

We both know what *this* means. *This* is more than friendship. *This* is an attraction.

Benoit says, "My first week in America has gone quickly. I hope the next one is slow. I want to enjoy every moment with you."

"Me, too."

His gray eyes are warm. He's leaning closer.

Our lips meet.

I feel like I'm melting.

When he finally pulls back, his cheeks are flushed. "I have been hoping for that."

"Same here."

We smile at each other. I snuggle into his arms, and we stay that way for a while.

Strange, but I feel like I'm falling a little more in love with him every day.

"I wish I could be the one to show you around the school," I say to Benoit the next morning at my locker. "I'd tell you the real deal. I'm sure you're going to have to ooh and ahh at the new gym and computer lab."

"I will make sure to ooh and ahh appropriately." He grins lazily. His hand is propped on the locker behind me, and he's leaning in to me. It's as if he wants to be kissing me right now, with all of these people around. I wouldn't object.

I smile up at him, and we share a zinger moment of attraction. He brushes his lips softly against mine. I want to deepen the kiss, but he's controlling this, so I submit to the sensual torture of his lips teasing mine. When it's over, I look away shyly, and my gaze suddenly locks with another pair of eyes across the hall. The intense look in Jared's eyes startles me.

Benoit follows my gaze, and turns back to me with a wry grin. "Your ex, perhaps?"

"Um, yeah. I don't see why he's giving me that look."

"You can't blame him. You broke his heart, can't you see?"

I'm not about to correct him and explain that Jared broke mine and that he has no right looking so pissed off.

Benoit gets dragged away by one of the exchange students just before the bell, and I head off to class. I can't stop thinking about the look Jared gave me. It was fierce—hurt, angry. Does he have a problem with me having a life after him? Or did I break some unwritten rule that you have to wait a year before you can kiss another guy in the hallway? I wasn't trying to rub Benoit in his face. And why should Jared care anyway? He broke up with *me*.

The more I think about it, the angrier it makes me. Would he prefer to see me sad than happy with a gorgeous Frenchman?

By lunchtime I've managed to put the matter aside. One look from Jared isn't worth crowding my brain space. Besides, Benoit has snuck away from the exchange students to join me and my friends in the caf.

He tells us about his morning tour of the school, and my friends laugh at his sarcastic commentary. I can tell they're impressed and a little awed by him. I bet they can sense the chemistry between us, the air around us crackling with electricity. He's certainly not hiding his feelings, since he's stroking my hair and rubbing circles on my back.

I am trying not to pay any attention to Jared, who's observing us from a few tables away. At one point I dart a glance his way, and our eyes meet. This time he doesn't have the angry intensity he seemed to have before; he looks…concerned. Does he think Benoit's going to take advantage of my vulnerable heartbroken self? I send him back a self-confident smile, letting Jared know, once and for all, that I'm just fine.

In fact, I'm better than ever.

While Benoit is off visiting the Statue of Liberty with the exchange students, I finish one of the guest blogs and send it off. Hopefully the blogger will post it fairly soon. Once I'm done that, I daydream about Benoit and find myself inspired to write a blog about chemistry.

Do You Believe in Love at First Sight?

The Oracle is too practical to believe in love at first sight, but the Oracle does understand how you could be intensely drawn to someone you don't even know.

Pheromones. Without even knowing it, you pick up on the scent of someone and your biology takes over. If the pheromones are just right, you will be fiercely drawn to this person, with all of your basic animal instincts wanting you to procreate with them.

There are a number of scented products that claim to simulate pheromones, giving people the hope that if their natural smell doesn't attract their crush, their new cologne will. The Oracle thinks that even though these colognes may catch someone's attention briefly, it won't be enough for a lasting attraction. So don't bother.

How can you tell if your attraction will be lasting? The kiss test, of course. A scent could briefly fool you, but not a kiss. A kiss puts you up close and personal, your pheromones mixing together, and you'll know right away if the chemistry is there…

* * *

That's the thing about time. When you're depressed, every hour is endless. When you're happy, time flies.

Mom and Erland were so right about the French guy being a distraction. I hate it when they're right.

Benoit and I have made the most of our two weeks. He's leaving tomorrow. It feels like he just got here yesterday.

"Richard's picking us up in twenty minutes," I say. "Are you ready?"

"I know you by now, Kayla. The question is, are *you* ready?"

I laugh. "No, I want to change."

"I suppose I should leave the room then?" His brows go up. He plays with it, this sexual tension between us. "I will be in my room. Let me know when you are ready."

Tonight's going to be awesome. Richard, a sophomore who also has an exchange student, has organized a bush party in Scrummer's Park. I change into a white tee and faded jeans— tight, but not so tight that I have to wear a thong. (Amy made me buy one last summer, but I never wear it, it's just too uncomfortable.) I put on some makeup and gather my hair into an artfully messy ponytail.

I look good. I guess romance suits me!

Richard parks behind the baseball diamond in Scrummer's Park, and we trek across the field to where the group has gathered. The French people kiss both of my cheeks. I've decided that French people are highly underrated. I don't find them snooty at all.

They describe the drama of their field trip to the Met, where one of the kids got caught smoking weed in the bathroom. Benoit's already told me this, but I pretend to be interested. I *am* interested—in the fact that his arm is around my shoulders.

Benoit's friend, Yann, arrives with a bottle of wine and plastic cups. We sip it in front of the fire pit, occasionally tossing branches in.

Evgeney comes up and sits beside me. I introduce him to Benoit. Evgeney has made an attempt at gelling his red hair; the gel makes it look greasy, but at least it controls the frizz. He tells a funny story about Mr. Granger freaking out in his history class, and we have a good laugh.

"How's it been with Guillaume?" I ask, seeing his exchange student across the fire pit chatting with a couple of American girls. From what I've heard, Guillaume hasn't been too enthusiastic about staying at Evgeney's.

"He is a bitch," Evgeney says.

I stifle a laugh. Did he just say *bitch?* I've never heard Evgeney curse before!

"I'm sorry you did not get someone better," Benoit says. "Guillaume gives French people a bad name. He is in love with himself."

Benoit pours a cup of wine for him. I like the way Benoit talks to Evgeney. That was one of the qualities I appreciated about Jared. He always treated Evgeney well.

Jared. I promptly shove him to the back of my mind where he belongs. Actually, he doesn't belong in there at all—and one of these days he won't be.

Evgeney leaves the fire pit around eleven, and Benoit and I drift into our own little world, surrounded by chatter and woodsmoke and music from somebody's portable radio.

At one point Benoit just stares at me. His eyes drift over every part of my face, and I don't feel a bit self-conscious. I feel like he's telling me I'm beautiful.

"You are an extraordinary lady, Kayla."

I giggle, because he called me a lady. "I'm glad you're here. I feel like I've known you—"

"Your whole life. Yes, I know. I feel that way, too."

And then he leans over and his lips brush mine, and we're breathing each other's breath, and it's like time stills.

"Beautiful." He pulls back, searches my eyes and kisses me again.

It's incredible, this guy's kiss. Intoxicating.

"I wish I could make love to you." His lips are drifting over my ear.

"Me, too. But I don't think it's a—"

"Shh, I know. Not when I leave tomorrow. Let us enjoy the time we have left."

The time we have left. It sounds so surreal. I push the thought aside—it doesn't even matter. All that matters is this moment, and I am going to live it to the fullest.

I'm not the only one who finds romance that week. When Tracey sets eyes on Iced Mocha, she is filled with relief and a double shot of happiness. He doesn't look just like his pictures. He looks better. Way better.

When he sees her, he gets up from the table where he's been waiting. He's maybe six feet instead of six-one, but he could have easily put his body type as muscular instead of fit. His skin is mocha, and his smile almost knocks Tracey off her feet. It's big and toothy and boyish. She wonders if he's feeling a similar sense of relief.

Could this be it? First time's the charm? One try at cyber-dating and she strikes gold?

Their hellos turn into a hug. She feels his arms tighten around her in the most delicious way.

One foot on the ground, says the voice in her head. (That voice, as she's told me, is *my* voice.) Alive with nervous energy, they approach the cash register to order coffees. As he reaches for his wallet, Tracey puts down the money. He seems impressed. It's part of Tracey's plan to show him she's not like other women, many of whom assume the man will pay.

They grab seats. Their eyes say a lot of things that their mouths wouldn't dare say.

"It's great to finally meet you in person," he says. "I've been feeling a little nervous, I admit."

"You're telling me." She's been having butterflies all week—and in the few minutes before meeting him, heart palpitations. "This is the first time I've met someone this way. It's a new thing for me."

"It doesn't matter how many people you meet, the nerves are always there. And the majority of the time it doesn't end up with the kind of relief I'm feeling now."

"Are most people not what you expect?"

"Let's put it this way—I've learned to expect the unexpected. It can make you jaded sometimes."

"Obviously you haven't given up hope."

His mouth quirks ruefully. "Two of my friends met their wives over the internet, so they keep the pressure on. Truth is, I'm a workaholic who isn't into the bar scene. It's a recipe for being single. So, no, I haven't given up."

Tracey knows that it wouldn't be hard for Mocha to meet women at bars. Maybe he's looking for a connection that goes beyond the physical. He's thirty-two, after all.

"You said you were a lawyer, right?" she asks, sipping her coffee.

"I'm an entertainment lawyer. I deal mainly with film options and contracts among actors, writers and studios. Sometimes I think I'm a slave to my BlackBerry, but I love what I do. You're in high tech?"

"Yeah, not nearly as exciting as the entertainment industry."

"You're in such a male-dominated field. I'm surprised you haven't been snatched up by now."

She recognizes the question: *why are you still single?*

"There are a lot of guys around, just not what I'm looking for. I guess you could say I'm selective."

"In other words, you don't want to settle."

"Exactly."

"I know what you mean. Most people settle, I think. And everybody wonders why the divorce rate is so high. It's ridiculous. If I'm lucky enough to get married, it's going to be for good."

She smiles. *A man after my own heart.*

I flop down on my bed with a big sigh.

Ah, whirlwind romance. It sweeps you up, leaves you suspended in the air and then lets go!

Mom and I just got back from seeing Benoit off at the airport. I can still smell his cologne in my room, still taste his lips. My palm tingles where he kissed it and then pressed it against his heart.

There is nothing about Benoit that isn't wonderful. For the two weeks he was here, I was in love. Love is such an awesome drug. I walked through the hallways at school with a big smile on my face, knowing I'd be spending the evening with Benoit.

All isn't lost though. I will visit Benoit as soon as I can save up the airfare. It will mean months of extra shifts at Eddie's, but it'll be worth it. At the latest, I could see him by Christmas. Will I be able to hang on to this precious feeling until then?

Yes. Absolutely.

I go to my computer and look at the pictures we took with his digital camera. God, he's beautiful.

Rebound.

The word pops into my mind like an unexpected hiccup.

ReBOUND.

Fine, I can accept it. Technically it has to be a rebound because Benoit falls within the timeline of my rebound equation. It doesn't matter, though. I'm sure many people find true love within a rebound.

I'm even thankful that Jared dumped me because otherwise my mom wouldn't have taken an exchange student to cheer me up, I wouldn't have met Benoit, and we wouldn't have had two wonderful weeks together!

Who knew that everything could work out so perfectly?

seven

36 Days into Rebound Equation

"So you've really never seen *Glamour Girl* before?" Amy asks Zink, who's joined us for our Sunday-night ritual. It boggles her mind that anyone our age isn't watching it religiously.

"I usually attend Sunday-evening services at my grandmother's church in Harlem," Zink says. "The choir is fantastic."

Wearing a crisp dress shirt and dark gray slacks, Zink looks like he's just come from Sunday services. Amy brings him up to date on the main storylines of the show—the love triangles, the sex tape, the drunken orgy—as Zink's eyes get wider and wider. Ryan and I exchange a suspicious look. Is Zink just putting on an act or does he really not watch this stuff? Heart transplant recipient or not, he's still a teenager.

Zink turns to Sharese. "I thought you said *Glamour Girl* was a coming-of-age show."

"I said it was a typical teen show." I catch a prickle of annoyance in her voice. "That means the characters all have some growing up to do."

"It certainly sounds that way." He crosses his legs, resting his hands on his knee. "I suppose it'll be entertaining to watch them find their way."

When the show's first scene shows a couple making out in a lavish hotel room, Zink gasps. I can't be sure, but I think I hear him mumble, "Trash." Which, I suppose, is right on the mark. Still, it's fun trash.

Zink and Sharese are sitting on the love seat, though I don't see much lovin' going on. Their legs aren't touching and they aren't holding hands. But then, they only started dating recently, and they're pretty religious. I wonder if they're going to end up wearing virgin promise rings. Amy would have a field day with that.

As much as my friends and I enjoy the show, we're enjoying Zink's reaction to it—or overreaction—even more. His nostrils flare whenever something outrageous happens, and he turns to Sharese to mutter comments. She nods and nods and finally shushes him. We all glance at each other, trying not to laugh.

On the commercial, Ryan dares to ask, "Whaddaya think, Zink?"

"I think it's appalling! You can see Satan in every scene!"

We all burst out laughing. We can't help it. Sharese's hands tighten in her lap, and I know she's pissed off. I just can't tell if she's pissed off at Zink or at us for laughing at him.

Zink rubs his chin thoughtfully. "Come to think of it, we could study this show in youth group. The whole gamut of sin is covered."

Ryan laughs. "You could have a quiz—spot the sin!"

Viv raises her brows. "I'm not sure that's such a good idea. Even if everyone can spot them, the show still makes sinning look like a lot of fun."

"Good point." Zink gives a solemn nod. "That may be what Satan wants. I'll have to talk to Reverend Fielding about this."

Sharese puts a hand on his arm. "Please don't. I don't want Reverend Fielding to know that I watch this every week."

Zink looks shocked. "You want to hide this from Reverend Fielding?"

"It's not hiding if we don't tell him everything."

"I'm not sure Satan would agree," Amy says, managing to keep a straight face.

Sharese and Zink are still bickering when the show comes on again, so we have to crank up the volume. Hmm. Bickering this early in a relationship isn't a good sign. Maybe they're not the match made in heaven we'd all hoped for.

The next morning at our lockers, I ask Sharese for the real deal. "How are things going with you and Zink? There were some fireworks last night." *Though not of the romantic kind,* I don't add.

She eyes me like she knows where I'm going with this. "They're fine."

"I didn't exactly get the lovey-dovey vibe from you guys."

"I know, but it's still early. Reverend Fielding says it could take weeks before I feel the spark. Sometimes you have to get to know the person first."

"You were talking to your pastor about this?"

"Friday night after youth group he asked me how things were going with us. I told him they're okay."

"Isn't it weird that your pastor's asking about your relationship?"

"A little."

"I hope he's not trying to marry you off or something."

"I'm sure he'd love to see us get married one day." She sounds less than enthused. "So you must be sad that Benoit's gone, huh? I heard you made out with him at the bush party. Heard there was some real tongue action."

The thought of the kiss brings a smile to my lips. "We definitely kissed, but the tongue part isn't true. Benoit would never French kiss in front of people. He's far too refined."

"Refined?" Sharese laughs. "I like that."

I see Jared walking in our direction. I catch his eye and he gives a halfhearted smile, drops his head and keeps going.

Sharese notices the exchange. "You guys don't even talk?"

"No. I've only heard from him once and that was by phone. I guess it doesn't suit him to talk to me in public. That's fine with me." Of course, it isn't fine with me, and Sharese knows that.

"Maybe he just doesn't know what to say."

"There's nothing *to* say."

"I saw the way he looked at you, Kayla. I think he still has a thing for you."

"Why should I care if he does?"

I don't, I tell myself.

I don't.

I check my email when I get home from school, even before I raid the fridge. I'm hoping to get a line from Benoit, but there's nothing. Oh, well, he just got back and is probably jet-lagged. I write him a nice email saying that I hope he had a great trip back and that I miss him.

After having a snack and watching *Oprah,* I go back to the computer, and find a new email.

Dear Oracle,

There's this guy at work who asked me out today. I'm excited because I've had a crush on him for a while. He recently broke up with a girl who works on the eighth floor and I've heard she's upset with him.

I want to ask this girl for the lowdown. It might be awkward, but they were together for more than a year, so she must know him really well. If he's a jerk, I'd like to find out so I don't waste my time.

Should I talk to this girl or not?

Just Wondering

Juicy question!

Dear Just Wondering,

The idea of a relationship reference is not a new one. It's natural for us to want to minimize the emotional risk of a relationship by doing a little fact-finding beforehand.

There are two things to keep in mind. (1) Is it fair to ask his ex about him? And (2) Will you be getting accurate information? Think about your own exes—what would you say about them? What would they say about you? Would you want the guy you like talking to them about you?

If you've heard that he used to beat her, or that he slept with every girl on the block, then it might be wise to find out the truth. But if you haven't heard that type of thing, then I don't think going to his ex will give you the real lowdown. Either he broke up with her and she's hurt and will say nasty things about him, or she broke up with him and will give you numerous reasons to justify her decision. Neither scenario is useful.

My point? Don't ask her. Go out with him. Trust your judgment. Proceed with caution as with any relationship. Have fun.

Cheers,
The Oracle of Dating

After sending my reply, I wonder what kind of reference I'd give Jared. *Great boyfriend until he dumps you without any warning!*

Damn, there's still a lot of hurt, and I guess there will be for a while. I bet when I'm eighty I'll still feel sore when I see his yearbook picture. The song had it right: "the first cut is the deepest." And if it weren't for Benoit, I might still be bleeding.

I'm not obsessed, really. Just because I check my email twenty times a day to see if I've heard from Benoit doesn't mean I'm obsessed. I can't imagine why I haven't heard from him. Is he sick? Has he been in an accident? Has his computer crashed? I've sent him two emails already—my limit until I hear back.

And then, almost a week after he left, he replies.

Chère Kayla,
Let us not make it something different than it was: two wonderful joyous weeks. Two weeks I will always remember.

If we try to stretch it, if we try to make it last longer, we will change it. Now it is beautiful. Let it always be that way!

I hope you understand, my lovely Kayla. You are one of the most captivating people I have ever met.

Benoit

I stare at the email.

Tears flood my eyes, blurring the words on the screen.

I'm in shock. How could he do this when we connected so well? It doesn't make sense. If our two weeks together were as great as he said they were, why not give our relationship a shot?

Wasn't I worth it?

It's so unfair. Despite the heartbreak I went through with Jared, I managed to open myself up to someone else—only to get shot down again!

Hours later, I've pulled myself together thanks to the latest season of *Dexter* on DVD and some Frosted Flakes. Luckily, Mom and Erland aren't home. I don't want them to see me like this. Knowing Mom, she'll blame herself since she arranged for Benoit to stay with us.

There is only one thing left to do: calculate my newest rebound equation.

How long did we go out? Well, he was here for two weeks, and we were pretty much together the whole time. So let's say fourteen days.

Now the equation:

14 days divided by 8 = 1.75
+ 30 because he dumped me = 31.75
Do I fantasize about getting back together? No!
Do I think it's for the best? No!
Total: 31.75 days before I can have another relation-
      ship.

That's ridiculous! That's half of my rebound equation with Jared, and we were together almost six months.

I play around with the equation, but it's no use. Because I got dumped after a short period of time, my own rebound equation has screwed me over.

No way. I'm not going to let this happen.

I realize I should have made up some rules to go along with the rebound equation: (1) The rebound equation *only* applies to relationships that last over one month. (2) Do *not* calculate a new rebound equation while you are still in an old one.

Which is what I did. I dated a new guy before the time allotted from my first rebound equation was up, and now I'm paying the price!

I call up Tracey. As always, she makes sympathetic listening noises. Then she says, "It's really not so bad."

That is not what I need to hear right now. "It *is*. I really liked this guy. I think I was partly in love with him!"

"I know. I understand why it hurts. But it doesn't sound to me like you've been dumped."

"Of course I have! He basically said he has no interest in keeping in touch with me. How is that not being dumped?"

"Being dumped is when someone who can be with you chooses to break up with you. In this case, Benoit couldn't be with you so he decided not to keep the relationship going. Remember Anthony? Maybe you don't, because you were ten at the time."

"I remember. He's that British guy, right?"

"Yeah. I met him when Corinne and I were backpacking through Europe. We managed to hold it together for a year. We only saw each other three times after that first summer and that's because he had a job and a little spare money. It was hard, Kayla. A lot of phone calls, a lot of tears. I've always wondered if it was really worth it. I think we should have left it at those initial ten days in London instead of trying to drag it out. It didn't work."

"At least Anthony gave it a chance. Benoit didn't even want to try."

"Think about it. How often would you have been able to see him? Once a year? You don't have any money to fly to France."

"I was willing to work extra shifts at Eddie's for him!"

"Look at it this way. You weren't dumped, you were

discontinued. He knew it would be too difficult to continue the relationship, so he thought he'd save both of you a lot of pain and end it now."

She makes it sound so logical, but my emotions rebel. "If he never intended to keep the relationship going, he shouldn't have let us get so close!"

"I'm sure he didn't mean to mislead you. Neither of you planned for this to happen, right?"

"Right, but I'm not good at falling in love and then acting like it never happened."

"You need to look at this differently. You had a mini-romance, and an ego boost at a time when you needed it. Appreciate it for what it was."

Over the next few days, the Benoit fiasco weighs on my mind. I tell no one of my shame, not even my closest friends. It's too humiliating to be dropped twice in such a short period of time.

Gradually Tracey's words penetrate my emotional bruising. Maybe she was right. Maybe Benoit was doing the thinking for both of us while I was riding on my emotions.

The question is: under what circumstances should someone embark on a long-distance relationship?

For answers, I go to my friends. Sunday night, when we've finished watching *Glamour Girl,* I tell them, "Benoit and I decided we're not going to try the long-distance thing."

Ryan splutters on his soda. "I thought you were crazy about the guy!"

"I'm sure we'd be going out if we lived in the same city. But there's no point in putting all our energy into keeping the relationship going when we'd hardly ever see each other."

"Wow," Viv says. "I figured you'd do everything in your power to keep it going." She looks at Amy. "You were right."

"Right about what?" I ask.

"I said that keeping the relationship going was pointless," Amy says. "I knew you'd figure it out for yourself."

"So you'd never have a long-distance relationship?"

"Not if I'd only known the guy a couple of weeks, like you and Benoit. I might consider it if I'd been with the guy a really long time before we separated, but I'm still not sure."

"You made the right decision, Kayla," Sharese says. "I agree with Amy. I'd only give a long-distance relationship a shot if I'd been with the guy for at least a year. Who needs a boyfriend you hardly ever see? You get all the drawbacks and none of the benefits."

"What if two people go to different colleges, far away from each other?" I ask. "Does that mean they automatically have to break up?"

"There's no point in trying to keep it together when you're starting college," Amy says. "Anyone who says they can be faithful during their freshman year is a liar."

Viv looks horrified. "That's not true. You're talking about yourself."

"I'm talking about most people our age. There's no way I'd go to college tied to someone back here."

"Say Chad joined the army—would you be faithful, then?" Viv asks.

"I'd never date a guy in the army."

"But your own cousin is overseas!" Ryan says.

"Yeah, and my mom makes me write him every month. Total pain in the ass."

Long-Distance Relationships:
Are They Worth It?

Oh, sure. A long-distance relationship seems so romantic. Months of longing, passionate reunions and more months of longing. But are you up for the work it takes to maintain it? And if you commit to someone who lives far away, are you wasting dating opportunities and life lessons at home?

The Oracle is not saying that long-distance relationships are a total mistake. But as a rule, you should only undertake a long-distance relationship if:

1. You have the cash-flow to see him regularly.

2. You have been together at least six months and therefore have spent enough time together to know that you are compatible.

3. You will not resent him for making you pass up other relationship opportunities.

4. He is as crazy about you as you are about him.

   You shouldn't undertake a long-distance relationship if:

1. You haven't spent a lot of time with him before your separation.

2. You haven't met him in person. Some people start courtships online and invest a lot of time and money, from phone calls to airfare, only to be disappointed when they meet!

3. You would like to date other people before tying yourself down to one person.

4. You do not have a plan to visit him in the foreseeable future.

   Choose wisely...

With my new perspective, I finally email Benoit. I'm glad I didn't reply until I had calmed down and was seeing the situation more clearly.

Dear Benoit,
I understand and I agree. I, too, will look back fondly upon our time together.
    I wish you well.

Kayla

I am beginning to wonder if everything that has happened to me dating-wise, good and bad, is happening for a reason.

Maybe others will learn from my experiences.

Now that Benoit is gone, a lot has become clear. While I was with him, I deluded myself into believing I was over Jared, but I never really was. I still have more than three weeks left in my rebound equation, and I am determined not to date anybody until it's over. (However, I reserve the right to change my mind in the extremely unlikely event that one of my favorite TV vampire hotties asks me out.)

In the meantime, one of my guest blogs goes up on a site called areateen, and I get twenty-two extra hits that day. I was hoping for more, but it's not bad. If even one of those people becomes a client—or even learns something from the website—then it's worth the time I spent writing the blog. And who knows how many friends those twenty-two people will tell about the Oracle? Word of mouth is key. It's just too bad I can't track it.

Finally I receive the question that teenmoi has chosen for me to answer. Teenmoi is the site of a blogger named Brandy. She emailed me saying that when she put out an open call for questions, she got more than forty.

Dear Oracle of Dating,

I have a problem. At first I tried to pretend it was just a coincidence that it happened more than once, but now it's happened again!

Several guys I've been attracted to have turned out to be gay.

My friends say I have no gay-dar. They say that the guys I go for are way too artsy and stylish to be straight. But what's wrong with being attracted to a guy who is cultured and knows how to dress? Do I have to go for some meathead sports fan just to make sure he's straight?

What's wrong with me that I can't pick up the signs? Could it be that I'm really a lesbian and that's why I'm attracted to gay men—because I want women without being aware of it? I'm so confused!

The last guy I dated, who recently dumped me, said that he was bisexual. He said I had nothing to do with it, but now I'm wondering if I'm actually turning guys gay.

Please help, Oracle!

Disoriented

I read the email a couple of times and make notes on the different issues I want to address. I'm a little surprised that Brandy chose this particular question because it hits on some touchy issues. Anyway, I have no choice but to tackle it head-on. My sister's best friend, Corinne, has encountered this problem on a number of occasions, so it's definitely an issue I've thought about before.

I take a couple of days to work on my answer, then send it to Brandy, who promises to post it the next day. I mention on my website that my next blog tour visit is tomorrow at teenmoi. I love this blog tour idea. Hopefully this one will get the Oracle lots of hits!

Dear Disoriented,

No, you are not turning guys gay. There's a debate about what makes someone gay, but I think it's simply the way a person is born. You have nothing to do with it.

You do have a valid concern though. If most of the guys you are attracted to are gay or bisexual, I understand why that would distress you.

I can't make this blog into "How to Spot a Gay Guy" because that would involve stereotyping. But ask yourself what attracts you to these particular guys, and what they have in common, and you might find clues. Here are two questions to consider the next time you are deciding who to date:

Has this guy had any girlfriends (romantic ones) before?

Do you feel real sexual tension between you, or are you simply attracted to him because you get along well?

Unfortunately, neither of these questions can give you a definitive answer, but obviously you have to do things differently than you've done before. There's no need to assume that every straight guy is a meathead or sports nut. Lots of straight guys are deeper than that! It might also be worthwhile to ask yourself what you have against guys with more traditional masculine interests.

None of this means you're a lesbian. If you're of dating age, you likely know your orientation by now. If you're unsure, think back to your first crush in grade school—was it a boy or a girl? The answer should tell you your orientation.

Good luck,
The Oracle of Dating

Later that night, I get a surprise: an IM from Jared.

InvisibleBassist: Are you busy?

HelloImAGirl: You changed your username.

InvisibleBassist: Yeah, well.

Dead air. Does he have something to say or what? He's the one who contacted me.

InvisibleBassist: How are you doing?

HelloImAGirl: Fine. You?

InvisibleBassist: I'm good.

Good? Does he have to be good? Damn it, I should have said I'm great.

InvisibleBassist: I just wanted to see how you've been. Anything new?

HelloImAGirl: I'm doing some guest blogs on different teen websites and I'm really excited about it.

InvisibleBassist: Cool. Kayla, last time we talked, you didn't give me a chance to explain why I haven't been talking to you at school. I thought it would be awkward for both of us.

HelloImAGirl: Speak for yourself. I could have handled it.

InvisibleBassist: Okay, you're right. I'm the one who's been uncomfortable. But it doesn't help that your friends stare at me like I'm Bin Laden.

HelloImAGirl: I'm sorry if they do that. Anyway you wanted to make a clean break and that's what you did. Don't worry, if I'd had something to say, I would have. I've moved on.

InvisibleBassist: I saw that. I'm glad for you.

HelloImAGirl: Somehow that sounds patronizing.

InvisibleBassist: It's not.

HelloImAGirl: Good. I have to get back to work.

InvisibleBassist: Wait, I just want to say I'm sorry I hurt you. I really am. None of this has been easy for me. I feel like I've lost my best friend.

HelloImAGirl: You dumped me as your girlfriend, but it was your choice to dump me as your friend, too.

InvisibleBassist: Yeah, but it's not so simple. There are still feelings between us, or at least, I still have feelings for you. It's not like there's a switch I can turn off. If we'd hung out as friends we'd probably end up making out.

HelloImAGirl: I can't BELIEVE you said that!

InvisibleBassist: You know it's true. We won't ever be just friends.

HelloImAGirl: Then why are you IMing me? Just to make yourself feel better about the breakup? I'm fine. You don't have to worry about me.

Oh, God. I don't sound like I've moved on, do I?

HelloImAGirl: I'm expecting a call from Benoit, and I've got a lot to do here.

I'm lying because I want to hurt him, just a fraction of how much he hurt me. But I can't hurt him, because he doesn't love me anymore.

InvisibleBassist: I'm sorry for bothering you. Go on being the Oracle and being amazing. I hope one day you'll forgive me.

He logs off before I can reply.

It isn't fair. I'm practically over him. And for some reason he randomly IMs me like this, and then I'm thinking about him again. Hurting again. Why does he do this to me? What does he want?

Forgiveness. That's what he wants.

Until I forgive him, he can't truly move on. And maybe... maybe I can't either.

It's about time I write this email and have it done for good.

Dear Jared,

I forgive you—if there's anything to forgive. And I truly wish you happiness.

Kayla

eight

46 Days into Rebound Equation

At lunchtime the next day, I eat quickly with my friends then go to the computer lab to see if teenmoi's posted my blog yet. She has, and she even blogged on it herself!

As I start reading, my eyes bug out of my head.

So as you all know, this girl who calls herself the Oracle of Dating contacted me asking to do a guest post—in other words, to get some exposure through my blog. I sent her one of your questions and here's her response. Could she have been more offensive? I wouldn't have even posted it, but I promised her that I would, and I always keep my word.

What's with the Oracle of Dating anyway? This girl (if she is, in fact, a teenage girl like she claims) actually charges for her advice. I would never charge for giving advice—I don't think it's right. And trust me, this girl's advice is NOT worth paying for. If you think her response on this question is bad, you can see worse on her website. But I'll save you the bother by telling you what's there: crapola. It's like she thinks teens have nothing better to do than constantly think about dating. Like there aren't bigger problems in the world than getting a date! And let

me tell you, there's no issue this girl won't write about,
no matter how frivolous. She's blogged on how to flirt, for
God's sake. Anyway, take a look at this Q & A and let me
know what you think.

The computer room spins around me. I've been set up!
Brandy must have hated my website from the beginning and
relished this opportunity to bash it. She gave me a controversial
question that she knew would get me in hot water.

And for her to say she posted it only because she promised
me—that's ridiculous! Anyone would prefer not to have their
blog posted than have it insulted publicly. This girl is such a
phony.

I don't think blogging about flirting is frivolous. Some
people really need the help. And I'm not claiming there aren't
more important issues in the world than the ones I deal with,
but most teens are into dating or want to be. Who does she
think she is anyway?

Obviously I didn't do enough research before contacting
her. I go to the archives on teenmoi, skimming over some
of her older posts, and there I see all the red flags I'd missed.
Snarkiness, apparently, is Brandy's strong suit. The snarkier
the post, the more comments she gets. How could I have not
seen this before? I'd noticed that she bashed some celebrities,
but it never occurred to me that she'd turn her venom on a
guest blogger. I was so wrong.

No responses have been posted yet. I can only hope her
readers will see things differently.

For Ryan, the most offensive part of working at Eddie's is
being forced to wear the blue polyester shirt. No matter what
pants you wear with it, no matter how you roll up the sleeves
or accessorize, you can never look anything but lame.

But in one heart-stopping moment a few weeks ago, it

all changed. He spotted Kate, a brand-new employee, who walked in with the shirt on, ironed to perfection over a white collared shirt. And he fell madly in love with her. At least, I think he did. Ryan rarely admits to crushing on anyone, but I can see it from the way his cheeks change color when he talks to her, not to mention the way he stares in her direction. He probably thinks Kate is out of his league, though, and he may be right. She's three years older than him and a student at the Fashion Institute. With silky straight blond hair, perfectly arched brows and flawless makeup, she is Ryan's ideal girl.

I've tried to ease Ryan into talking about his crush, but without success. Maybe he's got the right attitude. If you tell your friends about your crush, they'll encourage you to ask the person out, and you'll run the risk of rejection. I used to be all about self-preservation myself, before the days of Jared.

Tonight Ryan is gawking at Kate as usual. When he and I go on break, I casually say, "Kate's got great hair, hasn't she?" He nods, as if to say, *does she ever.*

I really wish I could tell him what's going on with my website, but of course I can't do that. When I got home from school, I didn't check teenmoi's site, figuring there'd only be a couple of comments. I won't know until later tonight how people are reacting.

Ryan interrupts my thoughts with talk of the Viv situation. "She's seeing Sandeep regularly."

"How do you know? She hasn't mentioned him." But I realize I've been so hung up on Benoit the last little while that I didn't even bring it up. Maybe I should have.

"She's not going to mention him because she knows what you'll say. I asked her flat out if she's seeing him and she admitted she's been having coffee with him. She says they're not dating, but it's so obvious he's pursuing her. He tells her she's gorgeous and brilliant and all that crap. There's no doubt about it—he's reeling her in."

Ugh. Poor Viv. "No decent guy would say those things to a girl if he still has a girlfriend."

"That's what I said. But she actually feels sorry for him. She keeps saying he's in such a difficult position. I told her it sounds like a pretty sweet position to me. I just hope she wises up before it's too late."

"Me, too," I say gloomily. "I don't want to see her hurt again."

By the time I get home, I'm downright scared to go to the computer. But I have to see what's on there, regardless of what it is. I turn my computer on, telling myself that it'll be okay, that it won't be as bad as I'd feared. When I click on teenmoi's website and scroll down, I see a ton of comments.

- The Oracle of Dating is full of shit! This is such a prejudiced answer! She's playing on every stereotype in the book about homosexuals. She should be ashamed of herself. Being gay is "simply the way you're born," huh? She makes it sound like a disease.

- The Oracle crossed the line. These people are sick and she acts like being gay is normal and okay. Hasn't she read the Bible?

- I think Disoriented is a man-hater. Maybe she was abused by her father and that's why she hates straight men. She should wake up and get some psychological help! The Oracle of Dating is too afraid to tell the truth.

The posts go on and on, and ninety percent of them are trashing me. I feel like I'm being punched in the gut. If it weren't so traumatic to read how horrible a person I am, I might find it funny that they've managed to find fault with everything I wrote, and for opposite reasons.

I bet Brandy's loving every minute of it.

I check my website, and my worst fear is confirmed. The Oracle-bashing has spread to my website, where I've gotten a slew of new blog comments. One person wrote "If you're looking at this website a virus will infect your computer. Stay away! I already lost half my files!"

Oh, no! I'm being slammed in front of my readers. I hope everybody can see that these people are being unreasonable. I spot a post that comes to my defense. It's from LostGirl, which means it's Viv. "The Oracle has done her best to answer a tough question. I've looked at her other blogs, and she is always fair and not prejudiced. I think you should all leave her alone."

At least somebody is on my side.

Stay calm, Oracle. Think. Think damage control.

The first thing I do is disable blog comments on my website and delete the most offensive ones. Hopefully this will die down soon, but for now, this is the safest option. I also remove the mention that I've done a Q & A on teenmoi—the last thing I need is for even more people to see the bashfest. As for the mud-slinging on teenmoi, there's nothing I can do about it. I'm sure if I emailed Brandy and asked her to remove the blog, she wouldn't, and she'd tell her readers that I'd asked her to.

I peek back at teenmoi, and wish I hadn't. Several more cruel comments have been posted. I force myself to stop reading them.

I can't believe this. In my efforts to expand the Oracle, I've brought on disaster.

"I saw the controversy," Viv says at our lockers the next morning. "Are you doing okay?"

"I hardly slept last night. I feel like I've destroyed my own business. Everything I've worked for is going down the toilet."

"I'm sure this'll die down in a few days."

"I hope so, but how much damage can these people do in the meantime?"

"I bet your website's getting lots of hits, at least."

"It is. Hundreds."

"This will get people talking about your site. Everyone will make their own decision as to whether you're legit."

"Good point. It's just really hard to have those nasty things said about me. I know that my answer wasn't perfect, but they're blowing it all out of proportion."

"Just be glad your identity isn't out in the open. Picture how you'd feel if everyone at school knew who you were."

"You think the Rainbow Club would come after me?"

"Or the evangelical club. That's the funny thing about this—everyone hates you for different reasons. It doesn't matter what you said or meant to say. They're twisting your words any way they want."

We go our separate ways at the bell. I try to pay attention to the lesson, but it's impossible. I keep thinking that when someone runs a search for the Oracle of Dating, they'll see the controversy on teenmoi right away, and some people will pass up my website because of it.

My fists curl under my desk. The worst part is that I feel powerless. I can't stop them from bashing me, and I can't possibly respond to all of the accusations. Part of me thinks I shouldn't give these jerks the satisfaction of knowing I've read their comments by responding in any way. Another part of me says I should write a response of some kind.

One thing's for sure—I'm too upset to make a decision right

now. Anything I'd write would sound defensive and angry. I need to take a day or two to figure out what to do.

The weird thing is, I find myself wishing I could talk to Jared about this. He always had this calmness, this Zen way of dealing with things, that made whatever drama I was going through seem not so bad. None of those dramas were anything compared to this one. The business I've worked so hard to build is being attacked, and I'm terrified that everything I've worked for is going to disappear. I can't lose my business, I just can't!

"I know who you are."

It's not the typical greeting Evgeney gives me when I walk into chemistry class, but then, he's not a typical guy.

"I know who you are, too."

"That's not what I mean." He darts a glance around. "I know what you do." His last words are a whisper. "And I think what those people are saying about you is unfair!"

He knows I'm the Oracle? My mouth opens, but only a stutter comes out. Finally I manage, "How do you know?"

"Your web domain is registered to you."

"It is? Oh. Was it that easy to find out?"

"For those who know where to look, yes. You can switch the registration to private, if you like."

"I'd better do that right away." The last thing I need is for the teenmoi haters to find out who I am and leave a dead fish on my doorstep. "Do you know how to change it?"

He nods. "Meet me in the computer lab at lunchtime. I'll show you. It's easy."

"Thanks—I'd really appreciate it."

Mrs. Moser describes what we'll be doing for today's lab and hands out worksheets. Evgeney takes charge, as usual.

Once the classroom is buzzing, I ask him, "How long have you known?"

"From the start."

"Why didn't you say anything?"

He shrugs. "You obviously didn't want people to know. The only reason I've told you is because I want you to defend yourself against the horrible things they are saying about you. Then anyone who sees the controversy can read your statement and know that you are the real thing."

I'm comforted that he thinks I'm the real thing. With all the people bashing me, it's impossible not to second-guess myself. "Maybe if I write a more general statement instead of trying to address all the accusations, that would work."

"Yes, that is a good idea."

He focuses on the lab for a few minutes. My mind is reeling. Was it weird for Evgeney to contact me online for advice when we're lab partners? Was he comfortable paying me when I'm a friend? I guess he must be, because he's been very supportive.

"I won't charge you for advice from now on."

"I want to pay you—I appreciate the attention you give to my concerns and that is a worthwhile service to pay for. You do not charge much, anyway."

"I certainly haven't gotten rich off the website. I was hoping the blog tour would help with business, but it looks like that backfired."

"The final outcome is yet to be seen. I believe your business will weather the storm." He turns to me. "That is the appropriate expression, right? Weather the storm?"

I smile. "It is."

I scarf down my lunch at my locker and get to the computer lab early to check my email. I cringe. Several of the emails are hateful. Some I delete based on the scathing titles. A few I open and delete after skimming the first line.

"Hi." Evgeney sits at the station beside me, pulling up a chair. "Checking email?"

I nod.

He must see my expression, because he shakes his head sadly. "Ignorant people. If you'd like, you can attach a virus to your reply. As soon as they open it, their computer will be infected. Would you like me to set that up?"

"No, I can't do that. It would just confirm to them that I'm evil."

"Your choice. Now if you go into your domain registration, we'll set up the privacy setting. It will just take a minute."

It really does take a minute, but I doubt I could've figured out how to do it on my own. "You're quite the computer genius, aren't you?"

He smiles. "I enjoy technology. If you like, I could modernize some aspects of your website. Unless you think your web designer would be offended."

"My sister set up my website. I'm sure she'd love it if you made some changes. What do you suggest? I can't afford to pay you, but like I said before, I could give you my services free of charge."

"It's not necessary for you to reimburse me. I'll do it as a friend."

"So why won't you let me give you advice as a friend?"

"I want to support your business. Also, I have a favor to ask you."

"Oh, yeah? And what's that?"

"I want to be a 'viable option,' as you wrote in that blog. There is a girl, a beautiful girl named Rose, in my ballroom dancing class."

"Ballroom dancing, huh?" I grin. "That's fun."

"It was your idea, Miss Oracle. You said I must join a class in something that I enjoy. Back in Bulgaria, many of us studied ballroom as children. Men do not appear as interested in it over here, but that could work to my advantage. I have always enjoyed dancing. And when I entered the class, there was my lovely Rose."

"Tell me about her."

"She's pretty and kind—most good adjectives you can think of would apply. She is quite shy, but when she dances, she is glorious. We dance together at every class. I think she likes me well enough. But she might just see me as a friend. That's why I need you to help me."

"What can I do?"

"You can come to the class with me. We were all given a free guest pass in case we'd like to bring a friend. You will give me status."

Status? I never thought of myself as potentially giving someone status, but I can see what he means. I'm mainstream-looking and fashionable enough. Evgeney's a bit more on the unusual side. If I show up to class with him and we're obviously friends, that could make him a viable option for Rose.

"I'm hoping that you will raise my market value."

Wow, he really does study my website.

"I'll do it. When's the class? I work three shifts a week."

"Wednesday nights. We can start next week, not tonight. You have other things to deal with right now—like defending your reputation."

When I get home from school, I see that the traffic on my website has shot to crazy numbers. Unfortunately, most of the people are haters, judging by the emails I'm getting. Well, haters or not, I've decided how I'm going to respond.

One statement and that's it, I tell myself. I'll post it on my website and on teenmoi, then I'll put this behind me.

The Oracle's Reply

I would like to start off by thanking Brandy for the opportunity to visit her dynamic website. I was given a challenging question and I answered it as best I could, drawing on my experience and intuition. It may not be a perfect answer, but I'm not ashamed of it.

I find it unfortunate that some people have misconstrued my words in order to make me seem homophobic, sexist and everything else. Have you noticed that you don't all agree on what my views really are? In light of that, don't you think you should reexamine what I was trying to say?

The Oracle believes in gay rights, so those of you who don't can still hate me. For those of you who think I am anti-gay, please reread the previous sentence. If you have suggestions as to how I could have replied better to Disoriented's question, please post them.

I can't address every criticism that has been thrown at me. That would take a long time and many people would want to continue to argue. It is time for the haters to calm down. If my words have offended you on a regular basis, you should not continue to visit my website. If my words offended you only in this one post, I hope that you will reconsider your assessment of me. But it's up to you.

That's all I have to say on this matter, for now and forever.

Peace,
The Oracle of Dating

When I finish the statement, I skim it for mistakes, then post it. I hope that people will take a chill pill so that I can get back to the important work of giving dating advice. It's scary putting the statement out there, knowing full well that some of the haters will trash it. But Evgeney was right; it's about me, not about them. It's about standing up for myself and not staying silent in the face of attack. And hopefully, within a short time, this will all be just a bad memory.

nine

51 Days into Rebound Equation

I'm not so lucky. Days go by, and teenmoi and her readers are still having a field day with me.

What could I have done to create this type of karma? Did I knock down an old lady while hurrying across the street? Or give a customer the wrong change?

I have Brandy to thank because she keeps blogging about my site and how awful it is. She even lifts quotes from it, taking them totally out of context. I wonder if that's legal. As I anticipated, she tried to cut down my reply but did a terrible job of it—Viv and Evgeney agree with me on that one.

I keep blogging as the Oracle, wanting to show anyone who visits my site that I'm moving forward and that I won't be addressing the issue again. In a moment of weakness, I create a Google Alert for "Oracle of Dating." To my shock, I see that a few other bloggers are now having discussions about my site. Though none of them are as nasty as teenmoi, a few of them obviously enjoy poking fun at my advice. A couple of brave souls dare to defend me and even compliment me, including chicgal, who I guest-blogged for a few weeks ago. Chicgal is a class act and I email her to let her know how much I appreciate her support.

When I receive my midterm grades from my teachers, I'm depressed again. My grades have slipped this semester, which most of my teachers are eager to point out, as if I've disappointed them more than myself. My friends tell me not to beat myself up about it because heartbreak isn't conducive to studying. That may be true for the first few weeks, but after that, instead of turning back to my schoolwork, I chose to focus on the Oracle's blog tour. And look where that got me.

I have no choice now but to get my butt in gear. Instead of hurrying home from school to be the Oracle, I've got to be the student for a change. I decide I'll stay late at the library when I don't go to Eddie's. And since I have a history paper due next week, I've got my work cut out for me.

When I get home around supper time Monday night, I find Mom and Erland sitting on the couch. His arm is around her, and he seems to be trying to comfort her.

"What's going on?" I ask.

Mom looks a little traumatized. "I made a very bad mistake."

My mind reels with possibilities. Did she hit someone with the car? Forget to show up at a wedding?

"What is it?"

"I…" Mom starts speaking, then shakes her head like she doesn't want to believe it.

"Your mother gave the last rites to the wrong woman," Erland explains.

"Alice Smith," Mom says. "How many Alice Smiths can there be in one hospital?"

Erland squeezes her. "It's not your fault, dear. You had no way of knowing it was the wrong woman."

"Well, she did tell me that her cancer was in remission, but I thought she was just being positive. So I told her about eternal life. Once I left I heard a crashing sound. Apparently she threw a vase of flowers across the room. She thought her family had lied to her about going into remission."

"Yikes." I bite my lip, and I realize I'm trying not to laugh. It's really not funny at all to think that an old lady, having just battled cancer, had been given the last rites by accident. Not funny at all.

"I should have warned you that there is a negative astrological transit right now," Erland says. "Jupiter is square Mars, which is a time of hardship and confusion."

"I could've told you that," I say, thinking of all the mess-ups in my life and my friends' lives lately. "Try not to worry about it, Mom. It could've happened to anyone. You're the best minister ever."

"Thanks, sweetie."

I go over and give her a kiss. Then I catch sight of Erland, whose face is rather pink. He's trying not to laugh, too.

Tuesday after school I stay in the library until five to five, when the librarian flickers the lights to let us know that he's ready to lock up. I'm packing up my books when I hear my name.

Jared has emerged from the back, where the study carrels are, and is looking at me with a startled expression. I know I don't often stay after school, but I don't see why he looks *that* surprised.

We walk out together, pushing the heavy doors and entering the deserted hallway. I see he's got a big black sketchbook under his arm. "Still working on the portfolio?"

"Yeah, I'm applying for scholarships at a couple more places, so I'm redoing my whole portfolio."

"The whole thing? But it was amazing."

"Thanks, but it wasn't enough to get me where I want to be. Anyway, these new drawings will be a lot more polished."

He's got a determined look in his eyes, as if failure is not an option. The Jared I'm used to is more laid-back than that, but I know he feels there's a lot at stake here. His dream is at stake. I can relate to that.

"Are you heading to the subway?" he asks. "We can walk together, if you're cool with that."

"Of course I am. I'm cool with you, Jared. You got that email I wrote you a couple of weeks ago, right?"

"I did." His eyes dart away, in the direction of his locker. "I just need to grab a couple of things."

"Me, too."

We get our stuff and head out the side doors. The sky has mostly cleared up after some earlier rain, and the late-day sun peeks out from behind the clouds. It's May, finally, and warm enough that I don't need my hoodie.

Something about Jared seems stiff, awkward, and so I start blabbering about random stuff to kill the silence. At one point he looks at me and says, "Your email sounded like a goodbye. Like you didn't want to talk to me again."

"I wasn't saying that. But I didn't hear from you for ages, and then suddenly you wanted to see if I was okay."

He rakes a hand through his dark curls. "I never meant to come across that way."

"You said yourself that you didn't think we could be friends."

"I didn't mean it like that. I want to be friends with you, I always have, I just never knew how. I know I screwed up royally."

"I won't deny you screwed up. But I think I can be friends with you now."

I know that "being friends" doesn't mean we'll be hanging out like we used to or calling each other often. When people do that, it becomes even harder for them to move on. I've had countless clients who claim to be good friends with their exes, and it usually ends up with one of them still pining for the other. As for Jared and me, I think we're saying we want to be friendly, and we don't want to avoid each other anymore.

"I know you've moved on, Kayla. I hope everything's going good for you."

"It is. I'm not still in touch with Benoit, but it was fun while it lasted. And the possibilities are out there if you know where to look."

"I'm not concerned for you. You can have any guy you want."

"You don't have to say that."

"I know, but it's true."

"Thanks, I guess." I smile, and he smiles back, and I feel the zing that was always there between us. That zing is the reason we can't ever be close friends again. Jared knows it, too.

"I've wanted to contact you lately," he says. "I saw what's been happening with that trashy teenmoi site. Those people are being really unfair to you."

"They're doing a pretty good job of destroying my reputation."

"Actually, they're not. They're making themselves look like idiots. You refused to stoop to their level. You've come across as classy all the way. Anyone with a brain is going to see that."

"Thanks. It's funny…when this happened I wanted to talk to you about it. You always had this way of calming me down and making me feel better about things."

"I wish you had come to me." He glances my way. "I've wanted to talk to you, too." He takes a breath as if he's going to say something else, but he seems to think better of it.

Suddenly the air is feeling heavy. I give an uncomfortable laugh. "Well, I was hoping the controversy would die down, but it seems to only have picked up steam. A bunch of different websites are scrutinizing me now."

"All that publicity's going to pay off eventually. Are you getting more clients?"

"No."

"They'll probably visit the site a few times before deciding to contact you. You always said that's how it works. Give it time."

"If I could get some new clients out of this fiasco, it would be sweet. Though I'm not sure a few more clients will make up for it. Anyway, I'm not desperate for more work at the moment. My midterm grades weren't stellar so I've got to hit the books hard the next few weeks."

"Your grades slipped?" He looks shocked.

"It's been a busy few weeks, especially with the blog tour and, you know, the exchange student."

"Right."

When we get to the subway platform, my train comes up within seconds. "Well, I'll see you."

"Yeah. I'll see you."

I step onto the train and sit down. I'm tempted to give him a little wave as the train pulls away, but I decide against it. I always used to do that, and I don't want him to misinterpret it. As I lean back and put on my iPod, I reflect on our encounter. Jared seems to be working hard to find a way to afford art school. I hope he gets where he wants to be. He deserves to be happy.

It was cool to hear that he's been checking my website and that he's rooting for me. It's a shame that we can't be as open with each other as we used to be, but at least we can cheer each other on from afar.

I'm pumped. Tonight I'm going to help Evgeney get the girl, or die trying.

Not only has he made some excellent tweaks to my site, he's been really supportive through the teenmoi fiasco. He's proven himself to be a true friend, and I'll have no problem talking him up to this girl, Rose. I only hope the plan works.

I meet Evgeney at the subway station and am pleasantly surprised to see he's nicely dressed in black slacks and a stylish button-down white shirt. True, he's overgelled his hair, but you can't expect perfection.

"You look great—and I love that cologne."

"It's Reckless. You recommended it on your site last month."

I wink at him. "True that."

As we ride the subway, we discuss a plan of action. I'm to come into the class as a friend of his, partnering him in a few dances. Of course, I'm to laugh at his jokes and generally seem to enjoy his company. And I'm to talk with Rose whenever I can, extolling Evgeney's virtues. He asks me to be subtle about it, and I promise that I will. I want this to work. Evgeney deserves a shot with this girl.

Once we have the plan ironed out, I ask him a question that's been bugging me. "What's with Eastern European guys and dancing? You watch those dance shows and it's like half the guys are from Eastern Europe."

"It's part of our culture to learn to dance—it's considered a masculine quality to be able to dance well. Here it seems it's mostly girls who take dance. Even in this class we're going to, it's mainly girls. I think a lot of people have become interested from watching the dance contests on TV. I wonder how many guys these days can sweep a girl across a dance floor in a waltz or dazzle them with a tango. None that I know except for me."

We get off in Soho then walk a few blocks to Dimitri's Dance Studio. Climbing the stairs to the second floor, we enter a large room with shiny oak floors and walls lined with mirrors. There's already music on and a group of people at the side of the dance floor. They're being entertained by a gorgeous couple spinning around the floor.

"That's Dimitri and his partner, Svetlana."

Dimitri, with his slick dark hair and lean tight body, looks like one of the professional dancers on *Dancing with the Stars*. I swear, how do people even move like that?

Before we gather with the rest of the class, Evgeney whispers, "She's the one with blond hair and glasses, standing by the exit."

I see her right away, and inwardly breathe a sigh of relief. My first impression of Rose: sweet and shy. Part of me was worried that Evgeney's crush would be a bombshell with whom he'd have little chance of getting a date. Rose seems like she'd be a good match.

I've read several studies which concluded that people tend to go for mates who are around the same level of good looks as they are. Gorgeous people tend to find gorgeous mates, average-looking people with the same and so on. The interesting part is that it's rare that people end up marrying someone who is more than a point or two different on the good-looking scale. Now, of course good looks can be subjective, but studies find that we tend to be attracted to people who look like us.

I've noticed the same phenomenon myself. Sometimes I'll see a couple holding hands on the street and swear they could be brother and sister.

"I see we have a guest today!" an enthusiastic male voice bursts out.

I was too wrapped up in my thoughts to notice that Dimitri and his partner had stopped dancing, and he'd zeroed in on me.

"What is your name?"

"Kayla."

"And what brings you here today, Kayla?"

"My friend Evgeney says it's a great place to learn to dance."

"Wonderful! Welcome, welcome!"

Dimitri comes up to me as if he's going to drag me onto the floor, but he just reaches out to bend over my hand and bow grandly. I'm sure Amy would love this, but the attention is making me uncomfortable.

He takes a few steps back, and in another grand gesture, opens his arms. "Today, my friends, we learn a dance that will call upon the romantic inside you. Some say it is the most intimate dance that can happen between a man and a woman, besides the dance that brings all life." Holy crap, is he talking about...? "The Viennese waltz!"

A couple of girls cheer and the rest of us shuffle our feet and wait for the demonstration. It's weird that I'm going to be learning the waltz, the most romantic dance, with mostly female partners. This could be a good thing for Evgeney, though. Being the only single guy (the three other guys have come with partners) ratchets up his attractiveness.

Dimitri and Svetlana do an initial demonstration then break down the specific skills: the footwork, the position of the arms and hands and the facial expression. We pair up, and Evgeney is, of course, my partner, though I know we'll be rotating partners soon. Dimitri's philosophy, apparently, is that it's best to learn to dance with a variety of partners.

The music comes on, and we negotiate the first few steps of the waltz. To my surprise, Evgeney is an elegant dancer. I can tell from the moment he assumes the posture. Why should I be so surprised? Evgeney wowed the whole school with his wild dance number at the Halloween dance. Obviously his talent translates into ballroom.

Every few minutes we rotate partners, and eventually I'm dancing with Rose. It's weird holding another girl this way, even though we're not superclose to each other. Dancing is so different now than it used to be. I bet in the old days girls learned to dance by dancing with each other.

Rose is as sweet and shy as she looks, not to mention a little socially awkward. She has more talent for dancing than I do, though, because she's as graceful as a gazelle while I'm stepping all over her toes. Thank God we're not doing the quickstep.

"No, no, no—watch us, Kayla!" Dimitri pulls Rose away from me and waltzes her around the floor. When he gives her back, her cheeks are flushed.

"Now you." Uh-oh. I have to dance with Dimitri. I do my best to get through the steps, and he gives a slight nod. "Yes, some improvement." Then he hands me off to Rose.

"You're doing really well," she says. "I think Dimitri's a little high on himself, to be honest. He's a great dancer but Evgeney's a better teacher. I think he belongs in the advanced class, but I'm glad he stayed with us."

"Yeah, Evgeney's awesome. It was so nice of him to bring me here. My boyfriend doesn't want to have anything to do with ballroom dancing." I feel a twinge of guilt at the lie, but I feel it's important to let her know that Evgeney and I are just friends.

"He's very nice." Her eyes dart away shyly, and I hope I'm sensing what I think I'm sensing. Normally I'm good at reading if someone likes someone else, but right now I have a vested interest that could cloud my judgment.

I switch to another partner, a girl named Naomi who, like me, is puzzled by the turns required for the waltz, and we keep knocking each other over and laughing. So much for my dreams of being a natural dancer gliding gracefully across the floor.

The class is mercifully only an hour and a half long. When it's over, I say to Evgeney, "Wanna get something to eat?" Then I ask the others, "Anyone up for some food?" And I make sure to look at Rose specifically.

"Sure," she says. And two other girls say yes, and one of the couples.

"Any ideas on where to go?"

Evgeney suggests a diner a few blocks away, near the subway station. As we walk there, I'm hoping that Evgeney will find a way to walk with Rose, but instead she falls into step with the two other single girls, and Evgeney ends up leading the way.

When we get into the diner, I know what I have to do: get Evgeney and Rose sitting together, or at least across from each other. When Evgeney is about to slide into the booth, I catch his arm and give him a look. He nods, understanding, and stands next to the table as everyone sits down. When Rose slides into the booth, he slides in next to her, then I get in after him. He flicks me a satisfied glance.

"I think the waltz is your dance," Evgeney says, and she giggles demurely. I turn away so as not to interfere with their conversation. Naomi's across from me, and we commiserate on how the waltz isn't our thing, although we wish it could be. We both agree that we'd do better in hip-hop lessons.

Evgeney and Rose seem to be getting along well, but unfortunately other members of the group keep butting in, making it a table-wide conversation. Oh, well. I can tell they're sitting quite close together. I wonder if their bodies are touching.

The group of us hang out for just over an hour, enough time to chat and get a milkshake or a burger. But since it's a school night, we decide to get the bills as soon as we're finished and head off.

Outside the diner, we go our separate ways, with most of the group going north, and Evgeney, Rose and I going into the subway station. Once the subway pulls up and they get on, I hang back, saying, "The R train is better for me." Evgeney looks puzzled, since he knows that isn't true. He tries to wave me in, but I just wave and step back from the platform.

The train pulls away, and I only have to wait a few minutes for the next one. I've got a smile on my face the whole way home. I've given Evgeney a great opportunity to get to know her better. I just hope he gets a date out of it.

ten

54 Days into Rebound Equation

"Well, did you?" I demand in chemistry class the next day.

"Did I what?"

"Get her phone number."

Evgeney grins. "I did. And then she asked for mine."

"Yes!" My exclamation is so loud that I get shushed by Mrs. Moser, and I have to resort to silent exuberance.

"You did an excellent job of making me a viable option, and I thank you for that." Then he looks at me pointedly. "But you shouldn't have stayed on the platform. It was dangerous, and I never would've forgiven myself if..."

"Give me a break. It was fine. There was a businessman not far away who I'm sure would've played the hero if someone had tried to mug me. Plus, I carry Mace."

"You do?"

"Well, no, but I've always planned to. Anyway, I did what I had to do to accomplish my mission. I doubt you guys would've exchanged phone numbers if I'd been there. So, when are you going to call her?"

"Tomorrow night. You mentioned on your website that a guy should call within two days to show he's interested."

"You're my prize pupil, you know that?"

He chuckles. "I guess I am."

I realize that if Evgeney calls her Friday night, I'll have to wait until Monday to find out what happened, and that's unacceptable. "Call or email me after you talk to her, okay? I want to know how things go."

"I will."

But it turns out, Friday morning in class Evgeney has an update for me. "Guess who called me last night?"

"Seriously?"

"Yes. And when I casually asked about her weekend plans, she mentioned she had plans on Saturday night but not tonight. She left me the perfect opening to ask her out for dinner."

I'd like to shout hurray, but seeing my teacher's eyes on me, I just pat him on the back. "This is totally freaking fantastic!"

Evgeney agrees.

That night, Tracey calls. "He's still on the website, Kayla."

"Uh-oh."

"I don't get it. I took myself off after dating him for a week—I was getting all these responses and I didn't want to date anyone else. But he's still on there."

She's talking about Iced Mocha, aka James. They've been dating for over three weeks and I thought things were going really well.

"Maybe he's not checking his account."

"I wish. It usually says at the bottom of the screen when the user was last active, but he made that invisible. So he could be on there every day and I wouldn't know it. Here's the worst part—he put up a new profile picture."

"Are you sure the default pictures don't change automatically?"

"I'm sure. He changed it himself. Why would he do that if he wasn't looking to meet someone else?"

"I don't have an answer. Did you tell him you saw it?"

"No. If I tell him I looked at his profile, he'll think I was checking up on him."

"Maybe he's curious to see what's out there, but isn't acting on it. Wait a minute—how long did you say he's been on there?"

"He didn't say, but it sounded like at least a year."

"So this isn't all new to him."

"No. And last week we had this conversation about dating other people and he said he's happy with where we are right now! What should I do?"

"I'll be honest with you, Trace. I think your intuition is right about this."

She sighs. "I know I'm right. It's just—I thought he really liked me."

"I'm sure he does like you. But he likes other people, too."

"Oh, God. This is a nightmare."

"It's not a nightmare. You haven't slept with him yet, have you?"

She is silent.

"Oh. I hope you were careful."

"Of course I was careful! Damn it, I want to cry! What the hell is he playing me for? Why would he talk about plans for our future together, and then go and change his picture!"

"I'll find out if he's playing you. I'm going to create a profile that no guy can turn down and see whether he responds."

"That's a bit underhanded." Tracey sounds reluctant.

"So what? You want to know the truth, don't you?"

"Yeah. I guess I do."

I log on and create my profile. I make myself a twenty-five-year-old lawyer and model. I post pictures of an obscure model named Amber. There is no doubt that any guy would jump at this profile.

I find Iced Mocha's profile and send him a "smile." This doesn't cost me any money. Now I'll wait to see what happens.

Within minutes, I'm getting instant messages from random guys. I don't reply to any of them.

Iced Mocha sends a "smile" back. And suddenly, *bling!* An instant message.

IcedMocha: Hi there, Amber. Your profile and pics blew me
           away. Are you for real?

I take a couple of minutes to reply. I want to keep him waiting.

Amber: I'm wondering the same about you. Entertainment
       lawyer? Went to Brown? So if you're really who you
       say you are, what firm do you work for?

IcedMocha: Douglas and MacKay. My name is James Dawson. You
           can call up the firm and ask for me, if you want.

Amber: Sorry if I'm not as generous with my info. My friends
       have warned me that you can't always trust guys you
       meet this way.

IcedMocha: Your friends are wise. I wouldn't expect you to
divulge any personal information until you've met
me in person.

Amber: Are you saying you want to meet?

IcedMocha: I am. What about Tuesday night around 8? Name the
place and time and I'll be there.

Amber: Thank you, Mocha. I'll think about it.

IcedMocha: Please do. Good night, Amber.

Amber: Good night.

I log off. There it is: the proof Tracey was afraid of.

Poor Tracey. The first time she goes online, she runs into
a master player.

He's smooth, that's for sure.

Well, I'm not finished with him yet!

I send him an email.

Hello, James,

I've thought about your proposition, and I suppose I have nothing
to lose, and possibly a new friend to gain. I will meet you Tuesday
night at 8:00 p.m., as you suggested. There's a new club on
Bowery and First called the Onyx. Meet me at the bar. I'll be
coming from a meeting, so it's possible I could be a few minutes
late.

Cheers,
Amber

I click Send. And with that click, I am sending James the
player to the raunchiest gay bar in the city, complete with a
live drag show starting at 8:00 p.m.

My work here is done.

Confused: Hi, Oracle. Are you there?

Oracle: Yes, I'm here.

Confused: I have a problem with my boyfriend. It's so embarrassing I haven't been able to tell anyone.

Oracle: You can tell me. What's the problem?

Confused: I've been going out with this guy for a month. He's totally amazing. I mean, he's kind, cute and has really good grades. Honestly, Oracle, I think he might be the guy I've been waiting for. But there's one problem. He has bad breath.

Oracle: Does he have it all the time, or just sometimes?

Confused: All the time. It makes me think it might be gum disease or plaque and that grosses me out. I don't even want to get close to him.

Oracle: Do you think he knows? Maybe his friends or family would have told him already?

Confused: I doubt anyone's told him, because he doesn't seem to know it's a problem.

Oracle: Have you been offering him gum or breath mints? Something that might give him a hint?

Confused: He doesn't get it. He only takes the mints half the time I offer them.

Oracle: Do you know if he sees a dentist?

Confused: I don't know. We haven't talked about it. Oracle, I'm so messed up right now. I really care about this guy, but I don't know how long I can put up with his breath!

Oracle: The man of your dreams won't have bad breath. So either this guy will fix his, or you'll find somebody else. If you really like this guy, I think you should broach the topic. I know it's the last thing you want to do, but you'll be doing both of you a favor. Sure, he'll be embarrassed, but in the end

he'll benefit from your honesty. Then he will either
do something about it or not. If he doesn't, then
you know he's not the guy for you.

Confused: You're right. I have to tell him. How do I do that?

Oracle: You could try something like, "Your breath's been a
little off these days. Have you changed your diet?"
If he says no, you can say, "Really? I wonder what
it is then. Maybe you should have it checked out."

Confused: Oracle, I don't know if I can do that. He's very
sensitive and he'll probably get upset.

Oracle: The alternative is to send him an email.

Confused: I can see doing that. I'll do it right now before
I chicken out.

Oracle: Good luck.

Confused: Thanks, Oracle. You ROCK!

The following Tuesday night, Amber gets an email from
Iced Mocha.

You set me up, you bitch! That place was disgusting. I'm going to
post a warning to all the guys to stay away from you. I bet you're
butt ugly and hate men. Probably because they all hate you!

I promptly erase Amber's profile, and just like that, I drop
off the site.

I'm glad that Mocha got a shock, but I still don't feel like
Tracey's been vindicated. The only good thing that came out
of this is that she could jump ship before she became even
more involved.

"I think you should keep looking online," I tell Tracey the

next evening when I visit her apartment, armed with pastries and soy decaf lattes. "Sure, you snagged a loser the first time around, but I've looked through a lot of profiles, and there seem to be some genuine guys out there."

"Seem to be." Tracey sips her latte. "Maybe I'm a poor judge of character. Before I meet someone else, I'll show you their profile."

"It's not your fault, Trace. Mocha's profile was perfect, especially the part about looking for a long-term relationship with the right woman. The guy's a classic con man."

"I don't understand guys like that. I'm glad he got manipulated for a change. Good job, sis."

We exchange a grin.

Later, as I'm riding the subway home, I'm wondering how many guys Tracey will have to date before she finds Mr. Right. I suppose that the more she dates, the higher her chance of finding the one for her. I feel a blog brewing. When I get in the door, I run upstairs to my room.

The More Dates, the Merrier?

Is the person who goes on fifty dates a year closer to meeting "the one" than the person who goes on five? Many singles believe that the answer is yes. The more bets they have on the table, the more likely they are to win.

Statistically, the Oracle agrees. And yet how can so many people be going on so many dates that are all misses?

Perhaps it's the thought that goes into placing the chips on the table that matters. Perhaps two or three well-placed bets are more effective than fifty random ones.

But how do you place those bets and win?

That's the million-dollar question.

The Oracle wants to know what you think. Which option best describes your philosophy of dating?

1. The more dates, the better. You've got to put yourself out there.

2. It's quality not quantity. You shouldn't have to date a lot to find the one you're looking for. It's all about how well you choose who to date.

I post the poll online, and within two days, I can see that the results are fairly split: sixty percent for number one, forty percent for number two. To me, these results aren't conclusive.

Perhaps it's simply a combination of the two—dating often, and choosing wisely.

When I hear about the house party on Saturday night, I'm a little reluctant to go. My last house party is one experience I'd like to forget. But, hey, am I going to let that stop me from having a good time? I wouldn't give Greg the satisfaction.

Viv is willing to go but, at the last minute, backs out when Sandeep calls her "in crisis." I take the bus with Amy and Ryan. Sharese is going to meet us there with Zink. Normally Chad would be with us, but he's on a week-long soccer tour in upstate New York. Amy doesn't mind. Her primary concern is getting ahold of some alcohol and getting the party started.

"That's all you brought?" Amy complains when Ryan reveals the bottle of rye he swiped from his parents' liquor cabinet. "Didn't they have a bigger bottle than that? That won't go far between three people."

"This was all I could get. If it's not enough, you can bum stuff off someone else. I'm sure that won't be hard."

"You're right…it won't be." Amy bats her eyelashes.

"I won't be having any," I say.

Amy frowns. "Why not?"

"Don't feel like it."

"Good, more for me!"

When we get to the party, it's just after ten. The venue, a Ditmas Avenue town house, has wall-to-wall carpeting and wall-to-wall sweaty bodies. I don't mind, because I hate walking into parties when there's hardly anybody there.

We head straight for the kitchen, where Ryan makes rye and Cokes in plastic cups. I help myself to some O.J. from the fridge. Then we go to the den and squish in with everyone. The music is so loud we can barely talk, but it doesn't matter because I'm enjoying the eye candy walking by.

I spot Sharese looking for us and wave her over. "Where's Zink?"

"Something came up...a family thing."

I can tell she's lying. Did they have a fight? Whatever it is, she's not volunteering any information.

Ryan and Amy don't seem to notice that anything is wrong. We're joined by a couple of jocks Amy has attracted. Both are cute and charming and remind me of that loser, Greg, so I keep my distance.

I discreetly ask Sharese, "Are you okay? Want to find some place to talk?"

She nods. I follow her into the kitchen, where she pushes some empty beer bottles aside and sits on the counter.

"Did you have a fight with Zink?"

"I wish. I did a terrible thing."

"What?"

"I told him I was staying home tonight. I hate lying, but I can't stand the thought of hanging around with him. I've been trying to give him a chance, focus on all the good qualities he has. But I'm not interested in him. I don't even like him."

"That's not a crime. I guess you'll have to find a way to break it to him."

"How can I do that? I'm the only girlfriend he's ever had

and he's totally in love with me. The whole church thinks we're the perfect couple!"

At that moment, Ryan walks into the kitchen. "Why'd you guys take off on me like that?" He looks at each of us. "Is something wrong?"

"I'm upset because I'm not feeling anything for Zink… except irritation," Sharese says.

I nod. "She has to break up with him."

Ryan is in shock. "You can't break up with transplant boy!"

"I want to, but whenever I try, he goes on about how much he loves me. And then he says he's scared his medication will stop working and his body will reject his heart."

"That's outright manipulation!" I say. "He can't guilt you into staying with him!"

"That's exactly what he's been doing. And I've let him get away with it."

"Give the guy a break," Ryan says. "You can't blame him for wanting to hang on to what he has. He's come so close to losing everything in the past."

I glare at him. "You're just making her feel worse."

Sharese turns to me. "See? Everyone thinks I'm the best thing that's ever happened to him. The problem is, I find him more annoying every day!"

"Maybe there's a way to get him to dump you," Ryan suggests.

"I've already tried that. Sometimes I'm a total bitch to him. But he doesn't seem to care. He's just happy to be with me."

"You're not doing him any favors if you stay with him out of pity," I say.

"I think he's happy to accept my pity."

"Okay, maybe he is, but you have to free yourself from him. It's not emotionally healthy."

"You sound like Oprah," Ryan says.

Or the Oracle, I don't say.

"I guess the longer I wait," Sharese admits, "the worse it'll be when I finally break up with him."

"Exactly. I know it's hard, but it's the right thing to do." I give her a hug.

"Where's Viv, anyway?" she asks. "She told me she was coming."

"One word," Ryan replies, "Sandeep."

"She said he called her really upset about something," I tell Sharese. "She thought she'd better see him."

"Are you serious? He always does that to her. What a drama king. He's as bad as Zink!"

"Zink only has *one* girlfriend, as far as we know," Ryan says. "I thought Sandeep promised to break up with that girl by now. Didn't the sister's wedding already happen?"

I shrug. "It's been more than a month. Viv hasn't said any more about it, and I didn't want to put her on the spot."

"If this goes on much longer, we may have to do an intervention," Ryan says.

The Oracle clicks awake. Relationship intervention, huh? I like that idea. If loved ones intervene for drug and alcohol problems, why not for bad relationships? I make a mental note to write a blog on it sometime.

We go back into the den to chill. Amy is still drinking beer with one of the jocks.

And Jared is sitting on the couch with Chelsea Yang.

Our eyes meet. His are very blue and very surprised to see me here.

My instincts scream *retreat!* and I back out of the room. Ryan and Sharese, seeing the situation, come with me to the basement, where a bunch of people are drinking and dancing.

Sharese is beside herself with bitchiness. "What's he doing here? He never goes to parties!"

"But Chelsea does," Ryan says.

I guess he'd do anything for his new girlfriend. She obviously has more influence over him than I ever did.

"It's no big deal, guys. Let's just dance."

They agree, though they seem surprised that I don't want to engage in a bitch-fest. People are dancing in the cramped space between two couches and a TV. It's dark and crowded, more a mosh pit than a dance floor. I don't care. I go wild to the music.

But my thoughts are chasing me. All of this talk about Sharese feeling too guilty to dump Zink makes me wonder how long Jared wanted to dump me before he actually did. Was he unhappy for weeks, even months? When I told him I loved him, was he cringing inwardly?

Damn it, somewhere along the line I stopped playing hard to get and made him the center of my life. That will never happen again. Sure, I will like a guy again. I will love again. But I will never let him know just how much I am devoted to him—unless we're married, of course.

We dance for a while, and manage to bum beers off a kid who is too drunk to care. I drink half a beer, get a little buzz going, and pass it off to Ryan. I know my limit.

Eventually we're all feeling tired, so Sharese calls her mom for a pick up.

"Let's find Amy," Ryan says.

We go back to the den, but Amy is nowhere to be found. Jared is still on the couch with Chelsea. I can tell he's drunk. His eyes are glassy. For the first time, I don't feel a rush of longing when I see him. He looks rather pitiful.

I walk up to him. "Have you seen Amy?"

"I think she went upstairs with that guy."

"Are you serious?"

"They were making out pretty heavy," Chelsea butts in, "so I told them to get a room."

"Why'd you do that?" Ryan demands. "She was drunk, and she has a boyfriend!"

"Amy conveniently forgot about that," Chelsea says. "She does what she wants to do, and it looks like she wants to *do* a lot."

We don't bother to reply, and head upstairs to find her. I'll knock on some bedroom doors if I have to.

But in the end, we find Amy on the landing on Bill Cohen's lap, giggling and stroking his face. She gives a big smile. "What's up, guys?"

"My mom's coming to pick us up," Sharese says. "That includes you."

"Okay, cool," she slurs, "I'm getting tired anyway." She kisses Bill on the lips. "Nice chilling with you, baby."

"Same here." He pats her ass as she climbs off his lap.

We all go outside to wait on the front steps. As soon as we close the door behind us, I blurt out, "What were you doing with him, Amy? What about Chad?"

"Chad's a sweetie." She yawns and puts her head on my shoulder. "I'm sleepy."

"More likely drunk," I mutter.

eleven

61 Days into Rebound Equation

I call up Amy at 11:30 a.m. and ask if she wants to meet for brunch.

"Sure, I need some greasy food," she says. "But if you want to chew me out or something, could you do it quietly, because I've got a headache."

"I'm not going to chew you out, but I think we should talk."

"Yeah, yeah. Can we go to Rocky's?"

We meet there at 12:30. She's looking a little rough, though I can see she took the time to shower, put on mascara and a comfy leisure suit with matching pink sneakers. We order the Big Breakfasts, complete with eggs, bacon, home fries and baked beans. Amy leans back into the padded booth. "Go to it, Kayla. Say what you have to say. I can see it bubbling inside you."

"Chad is such a nice guy. I don't understand why you'd disrespect him by making out with Bill."

Amy shrugs before taking a sip of orange juice. "Chad

won't find out. And even if he does, he'll get over it. I never promised him I'd be faithful."

"Don't you think he assumes you are?"

"He can assume what he wants. I wouldn't lie to the guy. I'm not like that."

"Just because you're not lying doesn't mean you're being honest."

"I see your point, but I'm only sixteen once. I think I'm entitled to have some fun. Sure, it's nice having a boyfriend, but it's not like I'm married or anything. I think you and the others take the whole relationship thing too seriously."

I open my mouth to contradict her, but the stats I know about teen dating flash before my eyes. Teen relationships are unlikely to last into your twenties.

So why do we take our relationships so seriously?

"No offense, but you and Jared acted like a married couple. Rather lame, if you ask me. All you did was get takeout and rent movies. You weren't as much fun when you were with him."

"I had fun." And where did that relationship get me but dumped? "Well, maybe I took it a little too seriously."

"You sure did. Think of how many opportunities you missed by being all about Jared! You never would've met that French guy if you hadn't broken up when you did, and he was only the beginning. Who knows what else is coming your way? Now is the time to play the field. My mom says I shouldn't settle down anytime soon."

I'm not sure that her mom would want her making out with random guys behind Chad's back, but it makes sense that she wouldn't want her to get too committed at this age. Mom and Erland had been concerned that Jared and I were getting too serious. Maybe everyone else was far smarter than I was.

"Let's face it, Kayla. Guys our age are so immature. If we

want something permanent, we'll be disappointed. Chad loves me, sure, but he probably loves his Xbox just as much."

The more I listen to Amy, the more I understand what she's saying, and the more disillusioned I become.

Is it a mistake for teens to take their relationships seriously?

I consider this question for the rest of the day, even while I'm watching *Glamour Girl* with my friends that night. By the time we're finished, I hurry home to write a blog.

Is Fidelity Pointless for Teens?
(In which the Oracle has a crisis of conscience)

Whatever happened to the days of dating for the sake of seeing what's out there? These days, just dating hardly ever happens among teens. If two people get along and go out more than once, they are usually considered a couple.

In our parents' generation, it was called **going steady,** and it was taken seriously, since some people actually got married out of high school. But **going steady** was usually an agreement that was formalized by one person asking the other: "Do you want to go steady?"

Today, becoming a couple seems to happen automatically, whether you're ready for it or not. And **going out** implies that you will be faithful.

Whatever happened to dating to get to know a broad range of people?

The Oracle asks you to consider: is it healthy to bind yourself to one person when you are a teen, even though the odds are low that you will marry your high school crush?

Of course, dating several people at a time can be complicated. If you really like one of your dates, you might only want to be with that person. And that's the problem here—if you really like someone, you won't want to see them date other people and you won't want to yourself.

One reason fidelity is important is that many teens these days are having sex. If you're having sex, you naturally want your partner to be faithful to you, not least because of the risk of STDs.

So that leads to the question: should teens really be having sex? Shouldn't they wait until they are older and have more stable, committed relationships?

I think teens should ask themselves if they're getting too serious too soon and closing off other avenues of opportunity.

Sincerely,
The Oracle of Dating

I post the blog. Then I wait. I have a feeling this will be one of my most controversial blogs yet.

· Within ten minutes, I get my first comment.

You don't know what you're talking about, Oracle! You don't sound like a teen, because if you were, you'd know that we can be as faithful and loving as any adults. Probably more! You should stop preaching at us. I bet you've never been laid anyway!
—Sheri, Atlanta, GA

She's right about one thing: I haven't been laid.

Over the next hour, I get a lot more comments. Obviously the teenmoi controversy really did increase traffic on my site. A debate starts in the comment section on whether teens should be having sex, which is funny considering the blog wasn't focused on that in the first place.

Although the debate is exciting, it's past eleven, and time for bed. I'm about to shut down the computer when an IM pops up.

InvisibleBassist: Hi, Kayla. Sorry to bug you this late. I wanted to say I'm sorry for what Chelsea said about Amy. She's very opinionated.

HelloImAGirl: Did she ask you to apologize to me?

InvisibleBassist: Yeah, after I told her she was out of line.

HelloImAGirl: It's not a big deal. I have a new perspective on Amy's cheating anyway.

InvisibleBassist: Really?

HelloImAGirl: Yeah. Why do we assume that teens have to be faithful and stick with one person at a time? I'm starting to think the idea is outdated.

InvisibleBassist: You can't be serious.

HelloImAGirl: I've broadened my perspective. I wrote a blog about it. You should read it.

InvisibleBassist: I will.

HelloImAGirl: Anyway, you can tell Chelsea not to worry.

InvisibleBassist: Cool. BTW Chelsea and I aren't going out. She's just a friend.

HelloImAGirl: You don't need to clarify things for me. It's none of my business.

InvisibleBassist: Okay. Well, good talking to you.

HelloImAGirl: Bye, Jared.

InvisibleBassist: Bye.

Weird, but when we close the conversation, I don't feel lost or let down. I actually feel...cool with things.

Could it be that I'm actually getting over him?

I glance at my calendar. According to my rebound equation, I'm supposed to be out of the rebound period as of tomorrow.

I lean back in my chair, a smile on my face.

Cafés—the perfect solution for the unathletic (like me), and for those who can't afford to shop every weekend because of insufficient cash flow (like me).

Here I am, sitting at the oddly named Coffee Café sipping my latte and realizing that I am by far the youngest person here. An old man is sketching me and it's weirding me out. I can hardly concentrate on *Women Who Run with the Wolves,* my attempt at reading something feminist.

Across the room, a bad date is going on. I wonder if they met online. The body language, at least on the guy's part, is totally standoffish. You don't need a Desmond Morris book on the human animal to see that. His eyes are wandering over the room and he's barely doing his part in the conversation. At one point he gets up and doesn't come back for ten minutes. When he returns, he's on his cell phone. You can practically see the steam coming out her ears. She says she has to go and quickly leaves—good, leave him in the dust, baby!

There's a thirtyish guy sitting behind a chess board trying to get someone to play with him. He asks an Arab guy, but his girlfriend doesn't want to part with him. I'd volunteer, but I'm not very good at chess and wouldn't be worthy competition.

The old man finishes his sketch and shows it to me. It's awful, but I tell him it's good. He smiles, but doesn't offer to give it to me. He flips the page and starts sketching someone else.

I scan the room. It's far more interesting observing people than reading this boring book. I study the couples and make a few notes about body language and what it says about a relationship. I'll have to blog on it sometime.

Uh-oh. My eyes lock with the chess guy. *Play?* he mouths.

I shake my head. *I'm not very good.*

Who cares? He waves me over.

Okay, fine. I pick up my stuff and sit on the chair on the opposite side of the chess board.

"What's your name?"

"Kayla."

"Josef." He's got a strong accent.

"Where are you from, Josef?"

"Romania. You are a student?"

"High school student, yeah." Just in case he's wondering if I'm older than I look—just to clarify that I'm not. "What about you?"

"I am an engineer." He moves his pawn.

I make a move, and then he does. It's my turn again.

"Are you sure?" he asks.

"Huh?" I'm holding my pawn midair.

He looks down at the board. "Are you sure you want to do that?"

It takes me several seconds to see that I was practically begging his bishop to kill my pawn.

"Oops. I don't want to do that."

He smiles. He's actually not a bad-looking man. If he'd get his eyebrows tweezed, he'd be cute.

I make a good move. I know it's a good move because he nods approvingly.

He makes another move.

I'm about to move my knight but he gives me a *don't-do-it* look so I put it back down and move a pawn. I know I'm supposed to approach the game with a strategy of some sort, but all I can think of is that I'm playing chess in a random café with a random older guy and I hope he doesn't secretly want to marry me and bring me back to Romania.

Soon I realize this will be a very short game even though he's helping me. Too bad he believes muttering "Think" will help.

A cute blond guy comes up, smacks Josef on the shoulder and starts speaking to him in another language. I'm taking a wild guess it's Romanian.

He looks at me curiously. "Sorry to intrude on your game." He speaks English like he was born here.

"No probs." I reach up to shake his hand. "I'm Kayla."

"Mikhail."

Mikhail. Michaela. It must be destiny!

I can't help but notice that he is not only very cute but around my age. He pulls up a chair and looks down at the board. "Who's winning?"

"Him," I say. "I don't stand a chance."

"You are a good learner," Josef says.

"You're a good liar."

We laugh. Mikhail has a loud happy laugh, and it makes me laugh more. I wish I could stay alive in the game longer because Mikhail and I have started getting to know each other. He tells me he's a junior at MLK high school.

"Checkmate."

I shake Josef's hand and pick up my stuff.

"Wait—you two can play," Josef says. "Mikhail is a beginner also."

I know I should object, since Mikhail obviously came here to play with Josef. But if he's not objecting…

"Beginner or not, you'll probably kick my ass, too." Then I wonder if I should use more refined language with this guy, since I'm trying to impress him.

But Mikhail laughs that great laugh. "We'll see, won't we?"

A couple of minutes into the game it becomes obvious that a) Mikhail is not really a beginner and b) Josef has deliberately set us up. I mean, Josef is now reading a book and ignoring us.

As for me, I'm paying far more attention to our conversation than to our chess game, which leads to a self-fulfilling prophecy: he kicks my ass.

I don't mind. I'm not the kind of person who thinks I'm good at everything, or even most things. What I am good at—advising people on dating and relationship issues—is what I should be using now to figure out how to see Mikhail again.

He declares checkmate.

"I hope you're not leaving because I kicked your ass." He's smiling.

"You kicked it all the way back to Brooklyn, Mikhail." (Oracle of Dating tip: people love to hear their own name.)

"If you want a rematch, I'll give you my email." He scrawls his address on a napkin.

Ding! Ding! Ding!

"I think I'll be wanting one." I fold the napkin and put it in my pocket. "Bye."

I walk out of the café, still hearing the bells in my head.

Ding, ding, ding! Jackpot!

"I did it. I broke up with him." Staring into her locker mirror, Sharese puts on some lipstick, then turns to me with a glum expression.

"I take it he didn't react well?"

She gives me a *duh* look. "At first he said he was going to stop coming to youth group because it would be too painful to see me. That made me feel horrible, so I said I'd leave instead. And he said that was a good idea."

"Are you serious?"

"Yeah. He knows I have a lot of friends there, but he doesn't care."

"He's trying to punish you for something that isn't your fault. You have to tell him you're not leaving youth group. You've been going there longer than he has, right?"

"Kind of. He was in and out of the hospital for years, so he wasn't there much. I can't use that as an argument, can I?"

"I guess not. What about staying away for a few weeks, then going back?"

"By then, the damage will be done. Zink's going to bad-mouth me to everyone."

"You think so?"

"I know so. I've heard the way he disses people. He can be vicious when he wants to be."

"You could talk to your minister and ask his advice."

"What's the point? I already said I'd leave the group. I doubt Zink would let me break my promise."

"You were under duress. Zink is a manipulator, heart transplant survivor or not. I think you should stand up to him. Show up at the next meeting."

Hi, Mikhail,

How are you? I've been busy with the usual: friends, homework, reading *Chess for Dummies*. How's your week been so far?

Kayla

Dear Kayla,

It's good to hear from you! My week's been a little crazy. I could write all the details here or we could meet for dinner Friday?

M.

Hi, M.,

Dinner sounds good. Call me to make a plan. 555-2425.

K.

Mikhail is a true Romanian gentleman, opening the door for me as we enter the restaurant. He's all confidence. If I were as good-looking as he is, I might be, too.

Not that I'm down on my looks. I'd rate myself somewhere between a seven and an eight-and-a-half, depending on lighting conditions and environmental factors. Tonight I'm wearing a turquoise sweater, a color that, I hope, cranks me up to a solid eight.

The hostess seats us. Mikhail gives me the choice booth seat while taking the hard-backed chair for himself.

We order sodas. The waitress leaves and there are a few beats of silence as we think of what to say.

"Have you been working on your chess?" he asks.

"Not so much. I'm not ready for that rematch just yet."

"So tonight's about checking out the competition?" He grins.

"Something like that." I grin back. "Anyway, you said you had a crazy week?"

"Yeah, two tests, plus four shifts at work."

"Where do you work?"

He bites his lip. "Can I tell you at the end of the date? I don't want to blow it with you, and girls don't react well when they hear the answer."

"Now you have to tell me. Is it some fast-food dive?"

"Worse. Much worse." I can see he's restraining a smile.

"What, you do coat check at a strip club?"

"You're not far off."

"Oh, no, you're a stripper!"

He laughs. "I'm not sure if I should take that as a compliment or not. But no, that's not it. I can't do fancy pec moves and I don't spend hours in a tanning bed."

I burst out laughing. "You've got to tell me, Mikhail. It's going to bother me all night."

"Okay, I work at Knockers."

"No way!"

"Yes way. I'm a line cook. Pays okay, and it's right around the corner from my house."

"Must be a lot of eye candy there, huh?"

"Sure, but the girls don't pay any attention to the kitchen staff except to bitch at us when we make a mistake."

"I know what it's like to have a crappy job. I work at Eddie's Grocery. It's the worst store ever. I'd never buy meat there because they leave it sitting in the back for hours."

"Yeah, a grocery store is probably the worst place to work. My ex works at Foodstop. If they're short-staffed, they don't even give her breaks. I keep telling her to quit, but she never listens to anything I say. She's very stubborn."

I catch the bitterness in his voice. Seeing my reaction, he says, "Sorry. It's just that she has a new boyfriend and it's been getting to me. She dumped me after two years because she said we were looking for different things. What the hell does that mean?"

Uh-oh. Ex talk. A first date no-no.

"When did you break up?" Maybe it happened recently and the hurt is still fresh. I can understand that.

"Four months ago. Wait—four and a half. You should see how ugly her new boyfriend is. I don't understand what she could possibly see in him."

Okay, this is seriously not an appropriate conversation. I have to change the topic. "Have you eaten here before?"

"Oh, yes, it's one of my favorite restaurants. Katarina and I used to come here all the time."

"Ah."

He must've caught the look on my face, because he says, "I promised myself I wouldn't talk about her tonight."

"It's okay."

"I'm glad. I feel like I can tell you anything."

From that point on, I feel like I'm his psychologist. He goes on and on about his ex, how perfect they were for each other, and how close he was to her family. I do a lot of nodding, but after a while I stop listening. I try several times to change the topic, but that's not easy to do when he's spilling his guts onto the table. The food, at least, is pretty good. I'll have to come back here sometime—without Mikhail.

Couldn't he just shut up and look cute? Is that too much to ask?

We must have been at the restaurant for three hours. Since he's talking so much, it takes him forever to eat. Just when I think he's finished, he orders coffee and dessert. Argh. I feel like my life is slipping away before my eyes.

Finally it's time to pay the bill. He offers to pay, but when I say I'll pay for myself, he doesn't insist. Damn the feminist in me—now this night is a total loss!

"Want to go to Starbucks?" he suggests as we get up. "I could go for another coffee."

"Sorry, but I really have to get home."

"But it's Friday night." He glances at his watch. "And it's only nine-thirty."

"Yeah, well, I'm tired."

He opens the door as I walk out, a far less impressive gesture now than when we came in. To my surprise, he goes in for a hug. I don't resist. I suppose the guy deserves a hug, if not a second date.

"It was great talking to you, Kayla. You're so easy to talk to."

I paste on a fake smile. "I've been told."

"Maybe we could get together Sunday afternoon?"

If you'll wear a muzzle, I want to say. Then, looking up at his eager face, I feel sorry for him. He deserves the truth.

"I'm sorry, Mikhail. I don't see this happening."

"Why not?" He seems genuinely surprised.

"I don't think you're over your ex." The understatement of the eon!

"Damn, I knew I shouldn't have talked about her."

"Don't worry about it."

"Why won't you give me a chance? Didn't you say I should move on?"

"Yes, you should." *Just not with me.* "Bye, Mikhail."

twelve

Saturday night, baby! The plan is takeout, gossip and whatever smutty stations we can intercept with Amy's satellite cable. Everyone is dying to hear about my date with Mikhail and Sharese's confrontation with Zink at the youth group last night.

"Did he freak out when he saw you?" I ask her.

"He ignored me at first, but then he started whispering about me any chance he got. I knew what he was doing because people kept looking at me funny. You'd be so proud of me, guys. I finally stood up to him."

"What'd you do?" We want to know.

"At the end of the night we all hold hands and bring up things to pray about. So I said, 'My wish is that we understand that there are two sides to every story and that we don't pass judgment on anybody. We should put an end to gossip because it's hurtful and unchristian.' Then Reverend Fielding went into a speech about how slander is a sin. I think it'll shut him up. He may be a manipulative jerk, but now he has the fear of God in him."

We clap for her.

"Now tell us about your date with the Hungarian guy!" Sharese says, and the focus shifts to me.

"He's Romanian, but it doesn't matter." I look at each one of them, building the suspense. "It was the worst date ever!"

Amy shrieks. "Oh, my God, did he vomit on you or something?"

"Uh, no. But he talked about his ex the entire time. He's looking for a counselor not a girlfriend."

Ryan groans. "I hope you told him where to go."

"No, but I told him there wouldn't be a second date. And I told him he wasn't over his ex."

Sharese grimaces. "That is so pathetic. I thought from what you said that the guy had potential."

"I thought so, too. He was cute, smart, but totally E.U." My friends know that I don't mean European Union, even if Romania is part of it, and I don't know if it is. E.U. means emotionally unavailable.

Amy says, "What a waste of time! Good thing you're rid of him." Which is ironic because we all know that in her relationship with Chad, it's Amy who's E.U.

"How are things with Chad?" Viv asks, probably thinking the same thing I am.

"Good. Same old." Her eyes narrow. "Are you asking me if he found out about what happened at the party? No, he didn't."

"You sound bored with him," Viv says.

"I'm not. I'm very happy with him." And she gives a big grin.

"If you want to keep him, go easy on the sexting," Ryan says. "There was a group in the guys' locker room checking out your pics."

"Really?" She doesn't seem displeased at all.

Viv stares at her. "You're not naked in them, are you?"

"Of course not. I'm just showing a little skin, that's all. It's amazing how the sight of a bra strap can drive a guy wild. The pics are just fun. They're not pornographic. Chad loved them. I told Bill about them, and he wanted to see them, too."

"Bill wasn't one of the guys in the room," Ryan says. "He must've sent them to someone else."

"So what? There's nothing in there I'm ashamed of." She looks at me. "If you do the same, I swear you'll have another boyfriend within a week. We just need to get you a push-up bra."

I cross my arms as if blocking her X-ray vision. "No, thanks."

Amy turns to Sharese. "What about you? You're rid of Zink now. You wouldn't even need a push-up."

"You're insane, Amy. If I ever took pics of myself and my parents found out, they'd freak. I'd be condemned to hell, or worse—they'd send me to live with my grandma in Georgia."

"Fine. Your loss."

"What about me?" Viv looks slightly offended. "You're not going to suggest I do it, too?"

"It's pointless to suggest it. You'd never do it."

"True, I never would. Never ever."

"But if you did, you could benefit from a push-up, too."

Viv rolls her eyes. "Thanks a lot."

We move on to another topic, but I suspect my friends are as troubled by Amy's sexting as I am. Not only is she putting her relationship with Chad in jeopardy, she's messing with her own reputation. She doesn't get it, though. She loves being the center of attention and wants to have endless guys after her.

When I get home that night, I decide to blog. It's late and I'm tired, but it has to be done.

Attention My Fellow Teens: A Warning about Sexting

So you take a cute picture of yourself in your slinky pj's, or while you're changing, and you know your BF or a friend of yours will get a kick out of it. They love the picture and send it to someone they know. And it goes on from there. Who knows how many people will end up seeing that picture of you? Maybe you're 100% sure your BF will closely guard the sexy pictures you send him. And he does. Until you break up, and he's mad as hell. Next thing you know, everyone at school's seen the pictures.

Some of you think that sending a provocative photo or sexy text message is the perfect way to flirt with a guy you like. It all sounds very innocent, right? It isn't. Because every time you send a picture or an explicit text message into cyberspace, it can come back to haunt you.

How do you know if you're going too far? Ask yourself this: how would I react if everyone at school were to see this picture, or if my parents or teachers were to read this text message? If the answer's that it would be a little embarrassing but not a big deal, fine. But if the answer's that you'd be totally humiliated, then that's your clue that you must STOP SEXTING NOW.

And for those of you who enjoy sending around pictures that were sent to you…did you know that distributing sexual photos of a minor is a criminal offense? In fact, some states prosecute these crimes as distributing child pornography and can make you a sex offender! So be careful!

The Oracle of Dating

Monday morning I'm dying to get to chemistry class to hear about Evgeney's date.

"So, how'd it go?"

Evgeney's expression gives nothing away. "It was a pleasant date."

"Pleasant? You're not smiling."

"The date was not quite what I had hoped."

My heart sinks. "Why not?"

"I realized that we are not as well matched as I'd first thought. She is a lovely girl with a sweet disposition. But there was something lacking."

"What was lacking? She seemed wonderful to me."

"I do not believe she's lacking in character. However, I didn't feel it was an intellectual match."

"But how do you know? Isn't one date too soon to assess someone's intelligence?"

"I am quite certain of my conclusion. Rose doesn't seem to be academically inclined. And she takes little interest in world issues."

"Yeah, but that's true of a lot of teenage girls."

"Certainly. But I know I am not compatible with someone who doesn't share my intellectual interests."

"Did you find out what her interests are?"

"Crafts of various kinds. I'm sure they require significant skill, and I appreciate the idea of having different interests than my girlfriend, but there must be some common ground. For instance, she did not realize that Bulgaria was in Eastern Europe."

"Ouch. Where did she think it was?"

"I didn't dare to ask. She also seemed uncomfortable when I attempted several different topics of conversation, such as politics, health care reform, the Catholic Church and classical music. It wasn't just her lack of knowledge of these things, it was her lack of interest. She is a very nice girl and I do not wish to hurt her feelings. Unfortunately she appears to have a significant affection for me." He gives me a pointed look. "Your strategy was very effective."

"I can't take credit for her feelings for you. She was already interested in you before I got involved." It really *was* too easy. I'm so disappointed that this hasn't worked out for Evgeney. I believed that he, of all people, would get the happy ending!

"Don't feel badly, Kayla. I don't. If I hadn't gone on a date with Rose, I wouldn't have known that we are not compatible. It was very worthwhile."

"I know. But is intellect really that big of a deal?"

He raises a brow. "Perhaps you should pose that question to the Oracle."

Evgeney is right, I decide as I'm sitting in my next class; the question of finding your intellectual match is definitely one the Oracle should explore.

I can't help but think of my relationship with Jared and how good an intellectual fit we were. We could verbally spar on any topic under the sun in a way that I found totally stimulating. On the surface, you might think we weren't well matched, since my marks were higher than his (except in art), but as we all know, grades in school aren't necessarily a reflection of how smart we are.

And a related question is: does a couple need to have common interests to be happy? Mom and Erland have religion in common, which I'm sure is important to them. But I'm not convinced you need to have the same interests as your partner as long as you have some common ground. You might even take pleasure in being with someone whose interests are different from your own, as long as you have similar values.

I'm sure Evgeney did the right thing by trusting his instincts and deciding not to string Rose along. For some people, a partner's intellect may not be important, but for someone like Evgeney, it's essential.

I stay late after school to work on a paper. It's around four-thirty by the time I grab my stuff from my locker. I notice that the lights are on in the art room. The door is closed but I peek through the glass and see Jared inside, painting. This room is where we first flirted and where we first kissed.

Jared looks up and squints at the glass. I'm not sure if he recognizes me from this distance, since he's borderline in need of glasses, but I figure I'll say hello anyway.

I open the door. "Hi."

"Hey, Kayla. What are you doing here so late?"

"Finishing an essay." I sit on a nearby table. "How's the portfolio going?"

"Great, I think. I'm almost done. I just have one more to paint after this. I want to show them I can paint, not just draw. They're looking for artists who can diversify."

"I hope it works out for you."

"Thanks." He looks at the clock. "I'm finishing up. Do you want to get a coffee?"

I blink. I figured we might walk to the subway together, but coffee? Well, he did say that he wanted to be friends. Coffee couldn't hurt.

"Sure."

I wait for him to pack up and we stop by his locker before leaving. We walk to the subway station, talking about nothing much along the way, and take the subway to the Tea Lounge, our old hangout. It has the same mellow, yuppie, granola atmosphere.

I order a soy latte and Jared gets a smoothie. We plunk down on one of the comfy couches, not hip to hip like we used to, but closer than we've been in a while. I remember those lips, how the bottom one is slightly fuller than the top. I know his smell, too—not cologne, but aloe deodorant.

It's strange, this distance between us. A part of me wants to lay my head against his chest and give way to nostalgia. It doesn't help that a romantic ballad is playing softly in the background.

Out the blue, he says, "You know, sometimes I wonder why we broke up."

We didn't break up—you broke up with me, I want to say. But I know it will sound bitchy, so I just give him a blank look.

"Sorry. I shouldn't have brought that up."

"It's okay. So how's Gina doing these days?"

"Business is booming. Even in a tough economy, transvestites invest in kinky clothes. Gina's taking a trip to Italy in August. Hasn't been in thirty years."

"That'll be great for her."

"Yeah. I know it'll be an adjustment for her when I move out in July, so it's good she has the trip to look forward to."

"You're moving out?" But I shouldn't be surprised. He always intended to move out when he turned eighteen, which happens on July 2. "I guess I didn't picture you doing it so soon after your birthday."

"There's no point in delaying it. I have leads on a couple of places. And some guys I know were talking about moving out of their parents' houses this summer, so that could work, too."

I know it's the right thing for him, but I can't help but feel sorry for Gina. He must guess what I'm thinking, because he says, "Gina won't get rid of me so easy. I'll still visit her."

I know he will. That's Jared, all right.

"This is fun," I say. "Like old times, huh?"

"Yeah." He smiles, kind of sadly.

I slap his arm playfully. "Stop. You're getting sentimental, I can see it."

"And you used to be the sentimental one."

Our eyes meet, and we have a moment. Time has always had a way of standing still when we look at each other.

I'm thinking that love never goes away completely—unless, maybe, it's replaced by hate. And despite the hurt he's caused me, the connection is still there.

I guess it always will be.

When I get home, my heart feels heavy. I know it shouldn't; Jared and I had a perfectly nice friendly time together, but the nostalgia is there. I'm inspired to post a blog.

On Having an Ex

Many people think that caring about your ex means you're hung up on them. I disagree. Once you love someone, really love them, you will always care about them, no matter how much time passes. You'll always remember, even if just a little, how it feels to know them deeply.

The reason so many people can't move on from their exes is because they believe that if you still care about your ex, you should get back together. That isn't always true. If you still care for your ex, it means you recognize that this person has enriched your life, even if they're not a part of it anymore. Consider that a blessing. Cherish the good memories...and leave it at that.

The Oracle of Dating

I know Jared might see it, but there's nothing in there that I'm ashamed of. In fact, I think it means I've come to a good place, where I can acknowledge that feelings are still between us, and be okay with that.

A few minutes later my phone rings. "Hi. I saw the blog."

"Hey, Jared. I guess you know what inspired it."

There's a long pause. "I'm about to send you an email. Feel free to call me after you read it."

"What's it about?"

"You'll see." He hangs up.

Within seconds, the email is in front of me.

Dear Kayla,

I've started this email a bunch of times in the past few weeks. Tonight I'll finally send it. It's time you know how I feel.

I'm in love with you. I never stopped loving you, not for one minute.

Somehow I talked myself out of our relationship. I blamed myself for relying too much on you. And when I didn't get that scholarship, I got spooked. I convinced myself that our relationship had distracted me from my goal.

Believe it or not, I never meant to break up with you. I needed some space, and tried to ask you for it, but before I knew it, things got out of hand and you were upset. Somehow I thought that I should just let it happen—that losing you was what I deserved for not working hard enough on my art.

You seemed to get over me so fast. Before I knew it, you were happy with another guy, and it killed me. But I felt I had no right to try to get you back since I'd screwed up so badly.

I've missed you every day since we broke up, and spending time with you lately made it even worse. I thought that missing you would fade over time, but it hasn't. I adore you as much as ever.

I don't know what I'll do after this year if my scholarship for art school doesn't work out. But the one thing I'm not confused about is how I feel about you. I'm sorry, so sorry, that I broke up with you. I needed time alone to figure out what I really wanted and what's really important: it's you, Kayla.

I want to get back together with you. Very, very badly. We can start fresh if you're up for it. Are you?

Love,
Jared

thirteen

"What the hell?" I say aloud. "You want me back? *Now?*"

I can't believe this. For weeks after the breakup, I dreamed of this. How can it take him two and a half months to decide that he wants me back—once my wound has closed and the scar is fading?

He has no right to change his mind, not when I've just confessed in my blog that somewhere, deep down, I still care about him.

Minutes pass, and I'm still in shock. I feel like he's reopened my wound and turned my insides upside down. All I know is I'm confused. Confused because there's a part of me that always wished he would come to his senses. Confused because I remember the feel of his hot mouth on mine, and I'm dying to experience that again.

Damn it, I have to shove that little fantasy aside. I can't take him back just because his kiss is—is pure erotic wickedness!

I call Tracey.

"You will not believe what happened, Trace. I got an email from Jared and—"

"He wants you back."

"What? How do you know?"

"It's well-known that this happens. I thought, as the Oracle, you'd know about it."

"I do know about it. I just didn't expect it would happen to me."

"Look, when a guy dumps a girl, he usually moves on right away. And then, months later, he realizes how good he had it with the first girl, and can't quite remember why he broke up with her."

"Whoa." She's right. It's a common formula. And yet I'd prefer to believe that Jared is unique in wanting me back. "I wonder if he'll change his mind."

"Not necessarily. It depends on how well he's thought this through. There's a possibility the relationship might not last the second time around, though."

I know that, too. I've even blogged on the fact that couples who get back together after breaking up are unlikely to stay together for long. The stats on that are clear.

"I was going to say no to him anyway, but hearing all of this makes it easier."

"Don't make any quick decisions. Obviously you're bamboozled by this. Anyone would be. Even though this is a known phenomenon, it doesn't mean he's not totally sincere in wanting you back. He probably is."

"If he'd changed his mind two weeks after the breakup, it would have been different. But now? How could he? You don't need to answer that. Thanks for everything, Trace."

"You're welcome. If you need to talk some more, just call."

We hang up. I know I should call Jared. But every time I pick up the phone, I slam it down again. He put me through so much, and all because he needed some space? And now he decides that I'm not the problem after all?

I already knew about the phenomenon of guys (or girls) blaming their significant other for their problems and breaking up with them. Now that he's figured it out himself, am I supposed to say that it's okay?

It's not okay. It's not even close to being okay.

The phone rings. Talk about not giving me time to think! "Hello."

"Kayla, hi." He sounds nervous. "Did you get my email?"

"Yeah. I wasn't ready to call you yet."

"Oh. Do you want to call me later then?"

"There's no point. I'm a little confused right now. Why would you put me through so much and then change your mind?"

There's a long silence. "I wish I'd handled it differently." His voice is soft and defeated.

"I wish you had, too."

"I don't blame you for being confused. I figured you'd be totally furious with me. Please take the time to think about it. Take as long as you want. I'm not going anywhere."

"What about Chelsea?"

"I told you that we were never together. She knew I was still hung up on you."

"If you expect me to jump at the chance to get back with you..."

"I never thought you'd take me back without making me suffer first."

I know from his voice that he's teasing me, but I'm not rolling with it. "You've hurt me a lot, but I'm not going to make this decision to get back at you."

"I know. You're not a vindictive person, and that's one of the reasons I love—"

"Don't say it. Please don't."

"Okay. But I do, Kayla. I hate myself for what I did to you. It was the biggest mistake of my life."

There was a time when I'd have done anything to hear him say that. But now?

I say nothing. There's a lump in my throat. I want to cry.

"Kayla, please think about it."

"I…I'll think about it." My throat is closing up. "Bye, Jared."

Three days pass. I don't dare tell my friends about Jared's offer. I know what they'll say and I don't want to hear it. I told Jared I would think about it, and that's what I'm doing. But I'm also trying my best to finish my term papers. How did June sneak up on me like this?

Is it just me, or is Jared spending more time than usual at his locker? He always looks like he wants to come over and talk, but he never budges. I guess that means he's leaving it to me. Although he always smiles, I can tell that he's worried. I'd like to put him out of his misery. Problem is, I have no idea what I'm going to do.

When I have trouble making a decision, I make a list of pros and cons. I suppose this situation isn't any different. So while I'm supposed to be listening to a lecture in English class, I make a list.

Pros:

★ I still have feelings for him.

★ He regrets breaking up with me.

★ I love being with him. I can be myself.

★ We have similar values and he's very supportive.

Cons:

★ He hurt me a lot. He doesn't deserve to have me back.

★ My friends are going to think I'm on crack if I take him back after what he's done.

★ Even if I still care about him, I really have moved on. Why should I go back?

★ It may not last. He could just dump me again the next time he's going through a hard time.

XoX

I stare at my list. Four pros, four cons. Then I find myself adding to the Pros: *He didn't really mean to break up with me in the first place. He just needed to reorganize his life and get his art back on track.*

This list isn't giving me any answers. I wish my decision was a clear one, but obviously it isn't. Staring at the list, I realize that what my friends think shouldn't be a factor in my decision. It shouldn't be, but it is. They've been trashing Jared ever since I broke the news about the breakup. How would they react if he's suddenly my boyfriend again? How would they treat him? And would they lose all respect for me?

Every time my eyes meet Jared's, I feel the electricity between us. It's almost as if he's purposely ramping up his sexual energy. I wonder if he's using witchcraft or he poured some aphrodisiac into my water bottle when I wasn't looking. How am I supposed to make a clearheaded decision when he has this effect on me?

I ask for the bathroom pass. When I get there, I'm stunned to find Amy, hair hanging over her face, sobbing over the sink.

I put an arm around her. "What happened?"

She looks up at me. Her face is red and her mascara has made two long stripes down her cheeks. "He found out about Bill at the party."

"Oh, no! How?"

"Bill told him. I don't know why. Chad didn't believe him at first, but one of the soccer players confirmed it. And Bill showed him the pictures I sent of myself. Chad freaked out. He h–hit him. The guys had to hold him back."

I don't know what to say. This was always a possibility, and Amy loved to play with fire. Still, I hated seeing it all blow up in her face.

"Chad broke up with me. I've never seen him so angry. He hates me!"

"Shh…it'll be okay."

"No, it won't. Chad's never going to talk to me again!"

"It's up to him how he wants to deal with this. You don't have any control over that. It may be time for you to move on."

"Move on? How can I move on when I love him?"

She loves him? That's hardly the type of thing I'd expect to hear from Amy, especially given her infidelity. "Are you sure about that? You've never mentioned loving him before."

"But I do love him! Would I have stayed with him for two years if I didn't?"

"I don't know. Would you have really made out with Bill if you were in love with Chad? I thought you were bored with the relationship."

"I *am* in love with Chad. I just didn't want to be, you know, restricted by the relationship."

"Look, I know this is hard for you, but you're not restricted anymore. I bet you'll be happier being single and getting to see what's out there."

"Single? Are you kidding me?"

Something clicks in my mind. Finally it's making sense— Amy, that is, the way Amy thinks. She wants the safety and comfort of a committed relationship, even though she finds it restrictive. She wants to be able to flirt and fool around with other guys and still have Chad right there waiting.

She could have broken up with Chad ages ago, but she always resisted, maybe because of her fear of being alone. That explains why she always needed the attention not only of Chad, but of other guys, as well. It also explains why she clung to Chad for so long even though it was obvious that she didn't love him the way he loved her.

Though Amy pretends to be blasé about relationships, I'm starting to think she's needier than the rest of us.

Over the next few days, we support Amy day and night. Between her tearful late-night phone calls and my own turmoil about Jared, I hardly get any sleep.

In chemistry class, Evgeney manages to brighten my day when he says, "I have a date this weekend with Naomi, another girl from my ballroom dancing class."

"Naomi? I loved her! How did it happen?"

"While we were dancing, she asked me to go to a movie this weekend." He blinks, like he's still processing it.

"Yay! So what do you think...is there potential with her?"

"I certainly hope so." He smiles at me. "I have you to thank."

"Me? Of course not."

"You helped me get the date with Rose. Once I went out with her, even though it did not work out, that made Naomi think of me as a viable option."

"You're giving me too much credit. I'm happy for you, Evgeney. You're a dating machine! Where are you taking her?"

"To a French restaurant called Avant Garde."

"Sounds classy. I hope it's not too expensive—you don't want to go over the top on a first date."

"Do not worry, I read your blog on that last year. One should not spend too much money on a first date. The prices at Avant Garde are reasonable."

I have to grin. "You know your stuff, Evgeney."

He grins back. "I have a good teacher."

That night I find myself sitting at the computer staring at a blank screen.

So many thoughts have been whirling in my head, it's finally time to write them down.

What To Do When He Wants You Back

It is practically a law of the universe that as soon as you are over the guy who broke up with you, he will want you back.

Is he doing it just to torture you? To rip away your newfound contentment and plunge you into a whirlpool of confusion?

Probably not. Not consciously anyway.

Why does he want you back now that you're mostly healed? Perhaps it's because you're the happy, self-assured, fun-loving person he liked in the first place. Now that you've dusted yourself off and have gone back to being who you were before the breakup, he finds you attractive again.

Of course, your ex will not always want to get back together with you. It's most likely to happen if a) the relationship was mostly happy, b) the relationship was codependent and he hasn't found anyone to replace you, or

c) he realizes you're the best girl around and besides, he misses you.

So what should you do? Run back into his arms like you've always dreamed? Go ahead, call him right now. Call him and tell him you'll take him back. Do it. Now.

Still reading? You had some hesitation then. You're wondering how long the relationship will last if you get back together. You're wondering if your friends will think you're totally whipped for taking him back just because he asked you.

The cold, hard truth is, if you get back together with your ex, it's unlikely to survive long-term. Is it worth it?

Whatever your decision, don't make it quickly. Don't make it out of the initial glee that he finally came to his senses. Don't make it out of bitterness because he dumped you in the first place. Take your time. Reflect and evaluate. A pros and cons list is never a bad idea.

And then do what you consider to be in your best interest long-term.

Peace,
The Oracle of Dating

I read it over a few more times, then post the blog. I'm trying to see the situation with Jared objectively. There is nothing wrong with taking back your ex as long as you have good reason. If you broke up because he abused you, or if you made each other miserable, then you shouldn't take him back. But what if you were happy?

Jared and I were happy. I could have that happiness again if I'd just say the word. So why is this such a hard decision?

Is it my pride? It's been known to rear its ugly head now and then. Jared bruised it terribly when he broke up with me, and I won't soon forget that.

But there's something else, a bigger reason.

It's me. I've changed. I'm not the same person he broke up with. I've been through a lot since the breakup, and I've grown from it. I think I'm even a better person from it. Wiser. I've seen the face of heartbreak, and it's given me a swift kick into adulthood.

If I take Jared back, will the newer, wiser me cease to exist?

A little while later, the phone rings. I was expecting this call.

"Hi. I saw the blog and I don't get it."

I hear traffic in the background. "Where are you?"

"Outside your house."

I go to the window. There he is at the bottom of the driveway on his cell. He waves.

"I'm not stalking you, Kayla, but this whole thing is driving me nuts. Will you take a walk with me?"

"Sure." I put on my sneakers and go outside.

His hands are in his pockets and his hair is messed up by the wind. I'm tempted to hurl myself into his arms, but I don't.

We walk.

"I wasn't sure if your blog was supposed to be your answer," he says. "If it is, I'm not sure what the answer is."

"It isn't my answer. It's just what I've been thinking lately."

"I figured that since you didn't decide right away, you might still have feelings for me."

"Of course I do. Just because you broke up with me doesn't mean I could automatically turn my feelings for you off."

"Look, I don't want to pressure you, but are you getting closer to a decision?"

"Sort of."

He stops walking and turns to face me, waiting.

"I'm not the same person I was when we broke up, Jared. I'm a lot more independent now. I don't want to throw all that away."

"How would you be throwing it away? You know I just want you to be yourself."

"I know that. If I reverted to the past, it wouldn't be your fault. It would be mine. But you have to know…second tries usually don't work. You've seen the stats on my website."

"I don't care about the stats, Kayla. We're not stats. We're not like everybody else."

"I would love to think so. But the reality is, if I go back to you feeling uncertain, I don't think it'll work. So what would be the point?"

I see the sadness in his eyes, and it breaks my heart.

"So your decision is no."

"My decision is that I can't make a decision right now. I'm not sure what I want. And I don't know how long it'll be before I figure it out."

His eyes hold mine. "That's cool with me. I'll wait."

"I'm not asking you to wait. I don't know how long I'd be asking you to wait for, and I can't guarantee what I'll decide. You should take opportunities that come your way if you want to. I will, too."

"I won't be taking any other opportunities. In the meantime, can we hang out as friends?"

"That's up to you. You're the one who said we wouldn't be able to spend time together without making out."

"I'm sorry I said that. I'll control myself if you want me to." He manages a smile.

"I do." I try not to smile because I want him to know that I'm serious. "Otherwise, we won't be able to hang out together."

"That's all the incentive I need. I'll take what I can get."

We start walking again. My nervousness is gone, replaced by relief. I'm so glad Jared hasn't made this hard for me. I'm glad he understands.

"It's such a nice night, Kayla. Want to walk up to Park Slope for a latte? As friends?"

"Sure, why not?"

As we walk, I glance at him, hoping that we really can be friends until I make my decision. He'd better not try to kiss me. Because if he does, how will I be able to resist?

fourteen

I decide to take an oath. Like doctors have the Hippocratic Oath, the Oracle, too, shall have an oath:

In order to fulfill my obligation as the Oracle of Dating, I must experience, not just observe, and use my experiences to grow emotionally and spiritually. I recognize that I may learn more from my failures than from my successes. My goals will be:

★ *to be wise without being self-righteous.*
★ *to use both sensitivity and logic in addressing problems.*
★ *to be compassionate and yet willing to challenge my clients when necessary.*

I, the Oracle of Dating, will seek what is positive and good in life for myself and for others. And when problems occur, I will not run away from them. I will face them with courage and determination and help others do the same.

Two weeks zip by. Projects are due. Exams are almost here. I'm updating my website as often as possible and fielding some annoying emails. It seems I'll never live down the teenmoi controversy. Thankfully, most of my clients haven't turned against me, and I've actually gotten a handful of new ones lately. I still don't know what the universe wants me to learn from this craziness. *Be careful what you say online?* I already knew that. *There will always be haters trying to bring you down?* It's not a pleasant thought, but I suppose it's true.

On the bright side, my hard work at school is paying off and my marks are improving. What a relief. School's something I'm good at, generally speaking (um, not including chemistry, math and art). Something I'm not good at? Making a decision about Jared. I was hoping that with time, an answer would come. But it hasn't. And I hate stringing him along, but what can I do?

Every day I tell myself to chill. So what if it takes me a month to decide, or two or three? He wouldn't want me to make a decision before I was sure, I know that.

Which doesn't mean he hasn't tried to influence me. Those hallway gazes are downright seductive. I'm sure if a Hollywood agent saw that hot, brooding stare, Jared would be cast in a rash of teen movies and I'd lose my chance with him forever. But it's not just his stare; a week ago he and The Invisible posted a new track on their MySpace page. It's a song called "I Let You Down" about a guy who screwed up, lost the love of his life and is trying to win her back. The song is sung by Tom, the lead singer, with Jared on background vocals and bass. It doesn't take a genius to see that Jared wrote it hoping to affect me. The first time I heard it, I was in tears. I've listened to it countless times, and each time I want to rush into his arms. So why can't I?

I still haven't told my friends about his offer. My only confidante is Tracey, but she's ultrabusy lately and hard to reach.

She usually gets like this when she's dating someone, so when I finally reach her over the phone, I ask her, "Are you dating someone new?"

She hesitates, then admits, "Yes."

"Why didn't you tell me?"

"I'm sorry, but I'm worried I'll jinx it. It's just that this guy is different from the others. We've only known each other for a couple of weeks and I don't want to get my hopes up yet. I'd prefer not talk about him until I'm sure it's going to be something real. I hope you understand."

"Of course." And I do, sort of. Nothing's ever worked out for her in the past, so she's trying to do things differently. She does tend to get overly excited when she meets a guy, only to have her hopes dashed. But I'm not used to her keeping anything from me. "Promise me he's not a salsa instructor."

"He's not. He has a perfectly decent job, I promise."

"And you're sure he isn't…misrepresenting himself, right?"

"I didn't meet him online, if that's what you're getting at. We were set up by a trusted friend who knows him well."

That alleviates my worries—a little.

But Tracey isn't the only one who's been elusive lately. It's about time I got to the bottom of the Sandeep affair, once and for all. So I make plans with Viv for a mani-pedi at our favorite inexpensive beauty shop.

"You haven't mentioned Sandeep in a while," I say carefully. I don't look to see her reaction, but focus on the pale pink brushstrokes on my fingernails. "Are you still hanging out with him?"

Viv's halfhearted grunt says it all. "He still calls sometimes, but I'm not going to make the effort to see him again. The wedding's long over, but he's dragging his feet about dumping his girlfriend. You were right about him. All of you were right."

I feel no satisfaction in being right about Sandeep. "You're going to find another guy you'll have a lot in common with, and he won't have a girlfriend."

"I'm sure I will, someday. But it's weird. Sandeep was totally convincing. I didn't think he was a player."

"That's the thing about guys like him. They don't necessarily mean to be deceitful. They're deceiving themselves, too."

"What a waste of time. Next time he calls, I'm going to tell him not to call me again. I've had enough. You know what the worst part is? It's that he made me feel sorry for him. He always said how he was in such a tight spot. How it was torture to be falling in love with me while still worrying about his girlfriend."

"I can't believe he used the L word."

"Me neither. Max wants to beat him up."

"Oh, really?"

She glares at me. "Don't say it like that. Max is just being a friend. We chat online sometimes."

"Do you still care about him?"

She nods, her expression softening. "Neither of us stopped caring. But until we graduate, there's no point in even talking about it. It's so unfair. If Max and I could have just been together, I wouldn't have had to bother with a loser like Sandeep. But sometimes I'm tired of being alone."

I couldn't blame her. Except for the few weeks she'd dated Max on the sly, she's never had a boyfriend. It isn't fair.

But then, in love and romance, is anything fair?

Do You Have "Best Guy in the Room" Syndrome?

It's human nature that wherever we are, we're aware of the attractive people around us. Say there are only two guys in your workplace. Those guys will automatically become more attractive to you because they're the only guys around.

My point is this: you might find yourself crushing on someone you wouldn't have been interested in otherwise just because you're with him on a regular basis. In fact, you may find yourself lowering your standards—or throwing them out entirely—just because he's the only guy available. This is especially true if you're not meeting new guys anywhere else.

Are you crushing on that guy in your workplace because you really like him, or just because he's there? Think about it.

When I finish the blog, I realize what I'm really writing about: Viv's situation. If she had several eligible Indian guys to choose from, I bet she wouldn't have bothered to listen to Sandeep's sob story. The problem is, Viv meets so few guys that meet her criteria that she became emotionally invested in him, even though he didn't meet her most basic requirement: being single.

"Something's going on between you and Jared, isn't it?"

I swivel around to face Sharese. "Why would you say that?" I can feel the heat rising in my cheeks, so I duck into my locker to grab my books, hoping she doesn't notice.

"You guys are always looking at each other, especially when the other one isn't looking. He stares at you like a lost puppy or something."

"Lost puppy?" I was hoping she'd say a sex-starved medieval warrior.

"Yeah, and you're no better. What's going on?"

I look around to make sure no one in the crowded hallway is close enough to hear. "He wants me back. A few weeks ago, he wrote me this long email saying how it was a mistake to break up with me and he wants me to give him another chance."

"Wow! Are you guys seeing each other in secret?"

"No. I haven't made up my mind yet."

"Why not?"

"What do you mean, *why not?*"

"I thought you loved him."

"I did. I mean, maybe I do, but…"

"So what's the hesitation?"

I stare at her. "I thought you hated Jared."

"I did, but only because he broke up with you. I liked him before that. I can unhate him again. Just say the word."

"So you think I should take him back?"

"Only if it's what you want."

"I don't know. All my instincts say to get back with him, but I don't trust those instincts anymore. I told him I needed some time before I could give an answer."

"You're not punishing him, are you?"

"I don't think so. I want to do the right thing. I want everything I've been through to mean something, not be put in the past and forgotten. Does that make sense?"

"Of course it does. And if you get back together with him, you won't forget what it was like when you'd broken up and you were trying to get over him. I bet you won't take anything for granted."

"Do you think I did before?"

"Not you in particular. I think most people do, though. They find that special person and it's all pretty straightforward.

Jared made a mistake by dumping you, but if you love him, maybe you can forgive him and put all that behind you."

"I forgave him a while ago. At least, that's what I told myself. But then he asked me to take him back, and now I'm all messed up again."

"You're afraid that if he did that to you once, he could do it again."

I don't say anything, but I know she's hit the mark.

That evening Sharese's words echo in my mind. Having been rejected by Jared once, I can't help but be afraid it will happen again.

I remind myself that I got dumped by a cute Frenchman within my initial rebound equation. That was definitely a double whammy if there ever was one. Okay, so maybe I've proven that I can take major rejection. But do I want to leave myself open to another one?

Is the chance to be with Jared again worth the risk?

And suddenly, finally, the answer is obvious.

I usually don't leave the house this late—it's past nine-thirty on a school night—but I can't wait any longer to get this off my chest. Mom and Erland aren't home, so I don't need to make an awkward explanation about where I'm going.

It's a humid night with a slight breeze, and I can taste summer in the air. I jog to the subway station, descending to the underground platform. My stomach is flipping over with nerves, and I tell myself to relax. I have to get this over with.

When I get to his house, I don't particularly want to ring the doorbell. It could wake Gina, and it would be awkward if she answered the door, considering I haven't seen her in so long. I wonder if I should throw rocks at his window to get his attention. It would be romantic, but I'd hate to damage the window. So, standing on the lawn, I use my cell to call his.

"Hello?" he answers.

"Are you at home?"

"Yeah. Where are you?"

"Outside your house."

"Seriously?" His voice hikes up, almost cracking.

"Yeah. Wanna come for a walk?"

"Déjà vu. I'll be right out."

Ten seconds later, he emerges from the front door, jumping off the porch and looking around. He spots me. "Hey, Kayla." He sounds slightly out of breath, as if he ran down the stairs.

"Hi. My answer is yes."

His eyes widen. "Yes? You'll take me back?"

I smile. "Yes means yes."

And then I feel his warm lips cover my smile, and our mouths fuse together in a long, breathless moment. When he finally pulls away, I'm downright dizzy. There was more I wanted to say but hormones have hijacked my brain.

He's hugging me tight, so tight we breathe together. God, it feels so good to feel his heart beating against my chest. This feels right. This *is* right.

Minutes pass without words, just holding and kissing each other.

"I was sure you were going to say no."

"I wanted to say yes this whole time, but something was holding me back. Fear, I think. I was afraid that if we got back together you'd break up with me again."

"I told you, I'm not going to do that."

"Not soon, you won't. But you can't promise you'll never do it. I don't want you to promise that. I can't say I won't change my mind one day either. Let's just be honest about how we feel. If we're having doubts, we have to tell each other."

"I'm sorry I wasn't more open with you before."

"No more apologizing, Jared. We're starting over."

"Okay. I won't apologize to you anymore. But I think I'd better apologize to your friends. Either that, or hire a bodyguard." He laughs. "Hey, did you ever hear our new song on MySpace?"

"Yeah." I squeeze his hands. "I bet you wrote it."

He smiles. "I hoped you'd figure it out. I wanted to sing it myself, but the guys voted me down. We all know Tom's a much better singer."

"He'd be more likely to win *American Idol,* sure. But your voice is far sexier."

His mouth curves up. "Oh, yeah?"

"Yeah."

He whispers the lyrics in my ear. *"I want you, I need you back in my life. Take me back, angel. Don't leave me here in hell."*

I shiver at his words and the feel of him so close. It's like when we first got together, this incredible electricity.

He pulls back, brushing a few strands out of my face, his expression rueful. "Maybe I wouldn't win an award for original lyrics, but I meant every word."

"I know." And I kiss him again.

The next morning, when Jared and I lock eyes in the hallway, I feel myself melt. But we can't approach each other for a good-morning kiss, since I haven't told my friends yet, and I don't want to startle them with the news. I have plans to watch a movie with them at Viv's tonight, so I'll break the news then.

Throughout the day, last night plays in my head like a romantic movie, complete with declarations of love and passionate embraces. Although Jared invited me in, I said no because I knew that once I got comfortable in his bedroom, it would be doubly hard to leave, and I didn't want to get home too late. We have plenty of time to get to know each other again, to get close again. There's no need to rush it. Not that thoughts of being in his arms don't excite me in an unholy way!

At lunchtime in the caf, I can feel his eyes on me, and I return his gaze when my friends aren't looking. His eyes are smoldering, and his smile is subtle and wicked. He's trying to drive me crazy, and it's working.

When I get home from school, Mom and Erland are both home, so I figure it's as good a time as any to tell them the news. I'm not as nervous telling them as I will be telling my friends, because they never bashed Jared after the breakup, and Mom even said once that she missed him. So I tell them, explaining how it happened and how I took my time in making the decision. Their reaction is to smile and give approval.

"If you're happy, we're happy," Mom says, and Erland echoes that with a nod. "Jared's welcome for any Sunday dinner. Just give me some advance notice so I can get a pie. We haven't had key lime pie in a while, have we, Erland?"

Mom and I will have to talk about that sometime. Boyfriend or not, this girl deserves her key lime pie.

I do a little yoga breathing, but it doesn't help. What does help, though, is that I know Sharese supports my decision to get back together with Jared and has promised to unhate him right away.

I expect a collective "Are you insane?" and I'm ready for it. Unfortunately, before I can work up the courage to speak, they put on a movie, so I have to wait two hours before I tell them. When the movie ends and Viv starts flicking through the channels, I say, "I've got news."

They turn their heads my way. I have everyone's attention.

"This is something I've thought through for weeks. It's not an impulse decision."

"You sound like you're going to have a sex change," Amy says. "Just tell us already!"

"Jared and I…"

"I knew it!" Viv exclaims. "I knew you were going to get back together. It was just a matter of time. Didn't I tell you that last week, Ryan?"

"You did. You saw it coming." Ryan turns to me. "How'd this happen?"

I tell them the story, emphasizing how Jared had just needed time to figure things out in the first place and never meant to hurt me. When I'm through, Ryan shrugs. "I guess we can forgive him. It's not like he cheated on you."

Amy bristles. "Are you trying to tell me something?"

"No. I'm just saying."

"How do you know he's not going to change his mind?" Viv asks. "We don't want to see you get hurt again."

"He might change his mind someday, but I don't think he'll do it soon. I know he's serious about this, so it's worth giving it a shot."

"Do you love him?" Amy asks.

"Yes."

"Okay then," she says. "I'll accept it. I guess he wasn't that bad."

"It sounds like he's matured," Sharese points out. "He's learned his lesson."

Ryan agrees. "He's seen the light."

Were they being sincere? I wondered. I thought they'd be

fiercely against us getting back together. "So you're not all against it?"

"Of course not," Viv says. "We're glad he came to his senses."

Amy adds, "If he breaks your heart again, I'll smash his kneecaps. You can tell him that. Then tell him welcome back."

fifteen

On Monday after school, I get an email with the subject line: An opportunity for you.

Dear Oracle of Dating,

I'm a contributor to *Seventeen* magazine and I'm very impressed by your website. It seems to have gained a following, not to mention sparked a little controversy! I'm writing to ask if you'd like to be featured as one of our cool teen entrepreneurs for our Back to School issue. The catch is, for this to be interesting for our readers, I feel we'd need to feature you—the girl behind the website.

Of course, this is all assuming you really are a teen giving advice to fellow teens.

Are you willing to give up your anonymity for a little publicity?

Please let me know within a couple of days either way. I'll need to book a photographer ASAP. Sorry for the deadline, but if it's not going to be you, I'll need to find someone else soon.

Warmest wishes,
Deb Cossell

Is this for real? I read the email twice, then run a search for her name. I find several articles she's written for various magazines, including *Seventeen*.

It's the opportunity of a lifetime. It's exposure beyond my wildest dreams.

And yet there's a catch. My anonymity. I'd have to give it up, something I've never thought of doing. Something I've never really needed to consider before.

Oh, my God. I have to tell someone. I call Jared.

"You won't believe it."

"Are you okay? You sound like you forgot to breathe."

"You won't believe who I just got an email from!"

"I have no clue. Don't make me guess."

"*Seventeen* magazine. They're doing a story on teen entrepreneurs and they want to feature the Oracle of Dating."

"That's great, Kayla! How'd they find out about you?"

"I don't know. But she mentioned the controversy on the site, so maybe she found out about it because of that."

"So all of that stuff you went through really did pay off."

"Apparently." I still can't wrap my mind around this. "But there's a catch. If they're going to profile me, she wants to use my real name and picture. She says anonymity won't appeal to the readership."

"Makes sense. Do you have a problem with that?"

"I haven't had a chance to think about it. Being anonymous is so…"

"Safe?"

"I was going to say easy. But yeah, it's safe. I can say what I want without feeling people will judge me personally."

"Isn't that what you said about that teenmoi girl—that she didn't have to be held accountable for what she writes?"

"That's a good point. It's just…this is scary. It's a risk, isn't it?"

"Everything is a risk. Getting up in the morning is a risk. You can slip and bang your head in the shower. But you're not afraid of risks, are you?"

"No. I mean, maybe. It'll just be so strange for everyone to know I'm the Oracle. Especially everyone at school. I'm used to flying under the radar, and I like it that way."

"Well, you're going to have to get used to a little attention. I know you can handle it. Think of it this way—putting your identity behind your words will give what you say more power."

"You're right but…"

"You always say 'but.' This is the opportunity of a lifetime. Go for it, Oracle. Now, I'm off work at nine. Can I stop in and see you after?"

"Sure."

We hang up, and I lie back on my bed, thinking.

Jared's right. Anonymity is a luxury I can't afford if I want to get somewhere with my business. My whole purpose is to help as many people as I can, and this article could bring me lots of new clients. I'd be a fool to let this opportunity pass me by.

I go over to the computer and press reply.

Dear Ms. Cossell,

I'm honored to have been chosen for your list of young entrepreneurs. Yes, I'm a teen—I'm sixteen actually. I will happily accept your offer to be featured in *Seventeen* magazine. Please let me know what I should do next.

Thanks so much!
Michaela Cruickshank

Over the next few days, I try to put the *Seventeen* thing out of my mind and focus on exam prep. I'm missing Jared, though. We've only hung out a couple of times since we got back together and it's driving us crazy. But it's probably a good thing that we're making a slow start. We don't want our relationship to totally consume us this time around. I've worked too hard on the Oracle of Dating—and myself—to go back to my BF-centered ways.

When Jared gets word that he's gotten a scholarship for full tuition to the Manhattan School of Art, we're both over the moon. Then he shocks me by suggesting we celebrate on a *double* date. He used to be anti double dates, saying that he didn't want to share my company with another couple. This one he's set up himself, and he won't tell me who the other couple is.

We arrive at the restaurant just after seven, met by the scent of paprika and garlic. Felena's is a well-known Spanish place in Brooklyn Heights, but I've never been inside before. The ceilings are low, the lighting from wall sconces is dim, and the walls are covered in mosaics. We bypass the hostess and look around for familiar faces. Jared told me that I know the couple we're meeting, but that's all he let me in on. If it was one of my friends or his bandmates, there'd be no reason to keep it a secret, so my guess is Evgeney and Naomi. Jared knows that I consider Evgeney my star pupil. Tonight I'll get to see him in action—if I'm right.

Jared isn't usually into surprises, but judging from the smile at the edge of his mouth, he's enjoying this. We don't spot the mystery couple in the front section of the restaurant, so we go up some steps into the raised section at the back.

"Maybe they aren't here yet," I say. And then, through a cloud of paella smoke, I spot them. Tracey and Rodrigo are next to each other in a booth, heads bent in conversation.

"You set them up!" I throw my arms around him. "That's so sweet of you!"

He hugs me back, then grabs my waist and pulls me to the side as a waiter comes through with a huge tray. As we get closer, I see Tracey nuzzle Rodrigo's neck. He brushes a lock of hair off her forehead and kisses her there tenderly.

Then it clicks. I mean, really clicks. Tracey and Rodrigo haven't just been set up tonight. He's the guy she's been dating; the one she wasn't ready to tell me about. The one she thought was too good to be true.

They look up at us, beaming. I'm speechless.

"Sit down, sis," Tracey says. "We'll tell you everything."

Rodrigo gives me a warm smile. "Nice to see you again, Kayla. I feel like I know you already, what with Jared and Tracey talking about you so much."

"Thanks." I sit down, reeling, but happy. Ridiculously happy. I turn to Jared. "How did you…?"

"Um, well, I set them up—the rest is all them."

"When?"

"About a month ago."

"Five weeks tomorrow," Tracey says with a giggle. "Not that we're keeping track."

"I most certainly am." Rodrigo squeezes her to his side. "Jared told me that women like to have an excuse to celebrate, so it's a good idea to have frequent anniversaries in the first year."

Tracey nudges him. "And I thought celebrating our anniversary last week was your idea!"

"Maybe it wasn't my idea, but I'm smart enough to know how to follow good advice. I take my cues from Jared, who's learned the rules from the guru herself. I told him to give me any tip possible to hang on to you."

"Why didn't you tell me?" I ask Jared.

"I didn't want you to know until you'd made your decision about me. I wasn't sure if it would work out anyway. It could've totally backfired."

"It almost did." Rodrigo slants a glance at Tracey. "She stood me up on the first date."

Tracey tosses her hair. "So I confused the Black Tomato and the Green Tomato. It was an honest mistake."

And from there the night's all chatter and laughter. I don't need to drag Tracey to the bathroom to quiz her on Rodrigo because all I need to know is right in front of me. He's crazy about her, and not in the flighty, temporary way of so many guys she's met. I can tell that something deep and wonderful is happening here—on both sides of the table.

When I wake up the next morning, I feel a flutter of nervousness. Tonight's the night I'm going to tell my friends that I'm the Oracle, and I have no clue how they're going to react. Telling them that Jared and I got back together was one thing—it turned out they'd anticipated that—but this?

To prepare them for the news, I send a text: *I have something to tell you guys tonight. See you then.*

I spend the day studying, which involves reading through my notes and making little cheat sheets. I don't take the cheat sheets into the exam, of course, but writing the material really small and in the fewest words possible helps me remember it.

The plan is to meet up at Load It Up, a so-called gourmet burger place, where no burger topping is too unusual. Part of the fun is outdoing each other with our choice of toppings. Ryan usually wins. Last time his burger was a triple threat, with peanut butter, bacon and a fried egg.

I'm the last one to arrive. They fall silent as I walk up. "Hey, guys."

"Hey," they all say, looking at me with sympathy.

"You said you had something to tell us." Sharese gives my shoulder a squeeze when I slide into the booth next to her.

"You shouldn't blame yourself," Viv says. "Most of the time when people get back together, it doesn't work out. At least you gave it a shot."

I stare at them. "You think this is about Jared?"

"So, if it isn't, what is it?" Ryan asks.

Amy claps her hands together. "I knew it—she's pregnant! Ryan, you owe me ten bucks."

"I am so not pregnant," I say. "I'm not even doing anything that could get me pregnant—sorry to disappoint you. My news is nothing like that. Um…you know that website, the Oracle of Dating?"

My friends nod around the table.

"I've got to confess something. I'm the Oracle."

I look around at my friends, whose expressions register varying degrees of shock.

"You're kidding," Sharese says.

Ryan doesn't believe it either. "Yeah, right. You? A fountain of wisdom?"

I clear my throat. "Yes, me. I'm really sorry to keep it from you guys, but when I started the website, I was so afraid it would fail that I didn't want anyone to know. And after that, I was embarrassed, I guess. I'd heard you guys making fun of it."

Sharese turns to Viv. "You knew, didn't you? That's why you started that Facebook group to bring back the Oracle when she went offline last fall."

Viv nods guiltily. "Kayla felt she had to tell me. It was the Oracle who gave me the advice to date Max secretly. When Kayla realized that her advice got me grounded, she confessed that she was the Oracle."

Ryan narrows his eyes. "I bet Jared knows, too."

"Yeah, but he guessed. I'd written a blog after our first date and he figured it out."

"So are you making lots of money?" Sharese asks.

I wish. "No. Just enough to keep going. Hopefully that'll change sometime."

"Hey, I've got an idea for you," Amy says. "You should let people put up profiles and find dates through it."

"I wouldn't dare. A site like that could get out of control. Adults could be posing as teens."

"Does this mean we're going to get free advice?" Sharese asks. "Not that I need it, but still."

"You get free advice already. I just didn't say it was coming from the Oracle."

"I don't get why you didn't tell us before." Ryan's obviously not sure if he should be mad at me or excited by the news. "I know we made fun of the website, but we wouldn't have if we'd known it was you." He pauses. "Okay, so maybe we would have, but we would've supported you."

"I know. I was too sensitive. But I'm not as sensitive anymore. My website's taken a lot of flack lately, and in the end, it's toughened me up. I'm not afraid to let people know what I do anymore." I realize that it's true; I really am ready for my identity to be exposed. "I'm proud of my advice, and I'm standing behind it."

It's a bright blue-skied day, and I'm having lunch on the school lawn with my friends. The sun feels good on my skin. I tilt my head back and let it reflect off my sunglasses. Jared is beside me, his hand entwined with mine.

My friends are chatting it up as usual. Evgeney is with us, too, having rolled up his sleeves to tan his pale, freckled arms.

As for Amy, she's getting less emo every day. She's no longer glancing over her shoulder constantly for a Chad sighting and breaking down when she spots him.

"Thank God we'll be seniors next year," Sharese says between bites of salad. "The junior thing is old."

"Soon we'll be off to college, maybe going our separate ways," Viv says.

"That's not for another year," Ryan points out, "and, hello, we'll be texting and emailing each other so much that we won't get any work done."

"Good point," Viv says. "I'll have to block you so I can study."

"You wouldn't."

"I might have to." Viv laughs.

I glance at my watch. "It's almost time, guys." I stuff the remains of my lunch into the paper bag.

"Time for what?" They all want to know.

"I'm not telling."

"She obviously arranged for someone from the yearbook club to take a picture of us," Ryan says. "Why else would she have told us to look good?"

"Don't we always look good?" Amy asks. "What's special about today?"

"You'll have to wait and see. In the meantime, I have an extra brush and mirror if anyone wants to put on the finishing touches."

Making a joke of it, my friends scramble to pretty themselves up, mockingly grabbing the mirror from each other. Evgeney, serious as ever, takes out a little mirror and runs a comb through his hair. Jared doesn't spare his appearance a second glance, but I insist on patting his hair down a little. The wind isn't helping.

Soon a black hatchback pulls up in front of the lawn. A guy with a camera gets out and looks around.

I run over to him. "Hi, I'm Kayla. You're Paolo?"

"Yep. Great day, isn't it? We can shoot you and your friends right here on the lawn. I assume that's the group over there?"

"Yeah."

"Nice spot with the trees behind you. Let me get set up. It won't take long."

I hurry back to my friends. "The photographer is here. He's from *Seventeen* magazine."

My friends gawk at me.

I grin. "It turns out *Seventeen* is doing an article on young entrepreneurs, and they'd like to do a profile on the Oracle of Dating. I told them my friends inspired me and asked if she could use a picture of the group of us."

Amy starts to hyperventilate, but Sharese talks her through it, assuring her she wore the perfect outfit. Ryan and Viv battle over the brush, but Evgeney intervenes by handing Ryan his comb.

Paolo watches us with amusement as he's setting up his equipment. He places me in the center of the group and says he wants us to lounge on the grass like we're chilling.

"How are we supposed to chill when we're going to be in a national magazine?" Amy demands.

After taking a couple of practice shots, Paolo adjusts the camera and looks through the lens. "Perfect! You guys look fantastic. I want to see huge smiles, people! Say *world famous!*"

"World famous!" we say together.

Snap, snap, snap. Paolo keeps shouting encouragement, occasionally telling us to shift position. It's not hard for me to keep my smile in place, because at this moment I'm really, truly happy. I've got great friends around me and a boyfriend I love.

I'm tempted to call it a fairy-tale ending, but the Oracle knows there's always more to the story. And senior year promises to be full of surprises...

★ ★ ★ ★ ★

A teen dating guru offers advice anonymously through her popular website, OracleOfDating.com, leading to tense situations and intense romance in these stories of friendship, love and angst in high school.

**AVAILABLE NOW
WHEREVER BOOKS ARE SOLD!**

HARLEQUIN
TEEN
on Facebook®

www.facebook.com/HarlequinTEEN

Be first to find out about new releases, exciting sweepstakes and special events from Harlequin TEEN.

Get access to exclusive content, excerpts and videos.

Connect with your favorite Harlequin TEEN authors and fellow fans.

All in one place.

**HARLEQUIN
TEEN**

HTFACEBOOKTR

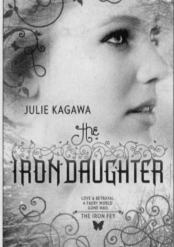